The Hypersleep Chronicles

Andrew Kraft

First Edition: March 2023

ISBN 979-8-3768-4781-7

DEDICATION

This book is dedicated to anyone who immediately looks up to search for the moon whenever their view of the sky becomes unobstructed. To those who dream about what opportunities lie beyond our closest celestial neighbor.

CONTENTS

Prologue

Stagnation
(Earth: Year 2302)

Advancements in technology had brought humanity far enough to present Isaac Jackson with this opportunity from Tarax Corporation. However, humanity had stagnated and this might be the only chance to keep people alive. Humans had already stifled the chance of expanding life throughout their current solar system through disharmony and their subversive ways. The only realistic way to keep life multiplanetary was to start anew in a different star system with a society focused on innovation and exploration instead of the gluttony and contentment that characterizes humanity.

The first problem with innovation in space travel was government regulations and control over the industry. Historically, less than one cent of every tax dollar was spent on space exploration, not nearly enough to make a difference. The government did everything with no sense of urgency; there wasn't an incentive to get things done efficiently and cost effectively when the only funding was extorted from taxpayers. Private industry was required for the advancement in space technology, and it had flourished in the early twenty-first century when the US started sending astronauts into space again.

It took a while to expunge the government shackles to lead the way for key innovations. As they traditionally did, governments impeded the expansion throughout the other planets and moons that might harbor life in their own solar system.

Earth's moon was covered in bases before the world's global superpowers could figure out regulations to enforce on other celestial bodies. This would eventually undermine the efforts to terraform and colonize any other moon or planet in their cosmic backyard. Governments couldn't agree on terraforming methods; who would lead the efforts, who would monitor progress, and just about any other matter concerning increasing their extraterrestrial footprint.

Who would ever want to leave the safety of their home when someone could have all the comfort and convenience money could buy? Biometric screening and health monitors in every corner of the house to ensure medical assistance could be requested in case of an emergency. Responsive climate control that kept a home perfectly comfortable during any season and customizable to fit anyone's exact needs. Standards now required an underground panic room in all homes, fully equipped to deal with most kinds of apocalyptic situations. These conveniences would seem to make the need for leaving the planet unnecessary. Those modern safety nets made Isaac sick.

Why wouldn't someone want to wait it out and see how long an individual could keep a great quality of life? While the human life expectancy expanded longer and longer, people just got lazier and lazier as they knew they had more and more time on the Earth. Isaac thought the under hundred-year life span was the perfect number to create a bit of urgency to produce and make the most out of the time spent in existence. Anything more than that created a complacency that continuously pushed out an individual's goals and accomplishments to the day after the next.

The population on Earth varied in the last couple of centuries. A huge environmental movement called for lower birthing rates to lessen the human climate impact on the planet. This led to a painfully slow collapse in society; there weren't enough productive citizens to provide for the continually aging population that survived longer as medical advancements continued. The movement would especially look silly as they learned more about carbon capture technologies and nuclear fusion generation that would combat their negative impact on the planet. This led to a rapid expansion in the growth of Earth's population as they needed to make up for these previous pestilent ideologies.

As one would expect, the pendulum would swing in the other direction. This overpopulation turned into an economic debacle as the rise of AI and robotics would displace the need for much of the workforce. Most manufacturing and even domestic needs around the house were now taken care of by affordable autonomous service robots. People relied on universal basic income and only the most ambitious of individuals notably contributed to society. Shipping people off to other star systems didn't seem like such a bad idea after all. This back-and-forth debate between overpopulation and underpopulation because of different ideologies was a tale as old as time and the ingenuity of humankind would always solve it.

Space travel had evolved to where decades and even centuries could pass as a spacecraft drifted through the vast unknown while the crew experienced no time passing in suspended animation. A spacecraft still could not go faster than 5 percent of the speed of light, which meant that suspended animation was necessary for a crew to make it anywhere within the reach of this transportation. Some would rather wait for a faster mode of travel to be discovered and become available. Isaac had a little more of a dreadful outlook on the abilities of humans on Earth.

Everyone had their own ideas of which exoplanets would be best to make a home given the current technology. However, Isaac knew his plan would succeed. They would find the perfect solar system to meet his three guidelines:

1. At least three planets could be terraformed. At least one move-in ready for humans. Most missions had left with the guideline of only needing two potential planets near their host star. This was certainly doable, but this

was not working out for them in their current solar system as many of them were trying to get the heck out. Moons in their current system like Europa and Enceladus could offer the opportunity for a place to live, it just wouldn't be the same as a planet. Many precious commodities would need to be imported and a lack of atmosphere wouldn't create an ideal environment for life as they were used to. If they were already going to be traveling around the galaxy, why not be on the lookout for an upgrade from their current situation?

2. No interference with an alien consciousness that had already developed. Intelligent consciousness was an ethical debate that throughout time had never had a concrete conclusion. There are many lines in which consciousness and intelligent life can be drawn. In some ways, plants communicate with each other. Other individuals would draw the line at an immune system. Some would say it's when a species uses tools like our ancestors long ago. If Isaac was going to convince a bunch of people into following him on a multigenerational space journey, it was best to make the line drawn at no interference with a developing consciousness on another planet at all. That parameter could be up for discussion once they arrived somewhere that checked every other box.

3. A star with a lifespan similar to the one the Earth rotated around. A star like their home sun would last about nine to ten billion years. Most stars have quite a long lifespan, however, the larger a star is, the shorter the lifespan it has. Larger stars may only burn on the order of

millions of years instead of billions of years. It would become alarming at the lengths of time it might take the crew to find their new home in the galaxy. With their current technology, a trip to the center of the galaxy would take them six hundred thousand years. A lot could change from the time a potential new star is first observed to when a crew travels along a long route of potentially hospitable star systems to get there.

The crew would rely mostly on imagery taken from orbit above the planet to make their decision on whether a planet could work for them. They also had a select number of drones at their disposal that they could send down to the planet to further examine the atmosphere and other details. This was mostly to be used in situations where they were certain that there was a serious potential for habitability; they didn't want to leave their foreign technology as litter on an alien world.

The crew would only have one chance at landing on a planet and setting up their base since they wouldn't have the ability to relaunch into space to find another home. There was no room for error once they decided where to land their spacecraft.

Chapter One

Isaac
(Earth: Year 2302)

"If everyone knew about this feature, no one would ever sign up to venture out into the galaxy, so it had to remain confidential."

-The Hypersleep Chronicles

It was terrifying and utterly fascinating to think when Isaac woke up in a week, everyone he knew and loved would have passed away. If there wasn't another launch cancellation due to weather or another unforeseen circumstance. One would think the people of Earth would have total control of the weather by now; some things just never seemed within reach. Isaac would wake up with a crew in a faraway star system after a long period of suspended animation and almost a hundred years would have passed on his home planet. In what seemed like going to sleep for only a night, from his perspective, billions and billions of normal folks would experience their entire existence. Each of these billions of people would spend their time circling around their home star tens or hundreds of times while he explored the infinite sea of possibilities in the cosmos.

Like a pappus from a dandelion, his crew would soon be among the many other missions to find another home in the vast array of stars in their galaxy.

Isaac looked out of his window as the frogs jumped around the only pond they would ever know in their lifetime. Light from the home star peeked through the trees and reflected off of the water into his room. Birds chirped in the distance as they relaxed in the birdhouses that Isaac had previously put up around the yard. The deer were getting a few sips of water, not knowing about the hunters lurking in the trees off in the distance. He couldn't get used to this since he'd be trapped on a ship with artificial light and no earthly pleasures surrounding him for a very long time.

"House, turn windows to transparent mode," Isaac requested.

The brick wall that lined the alley outside of his bedroom came into view. That was more like it. He might as well get used to this lack of scenery, considering the ambiguity of the views during his brief stops drifting through space for an uncertain amount of time. He already had a simple design scheme throughout his house. Mostly different shades of gray. There wasn't much effort involved in matching his heather gray sheets to the agreeable gray paint on the walls that went with the medium gray curtains. The black dressers and bed frame pulled everything together just right. He never felt the need to match different colors and create themes throughout the living space. It seemed like a waste of time to Isaac and this was only a temporary situation until he could be out among the stars in the equally droll spaceship interior.

The walk down his hallway featured all of his favorite events throughout history that inspired him to embark on this mission. The first frame he passed was a looping video of JFK's 1962 speech where JFK decreed, "We choose to go to the moon in this decade and do the other things, not because they are easy, but because they are hard." This embodied the very first space race, words to live by every day, and it gave him chills every time he walked by it. Next was a framed video of the first time two reusable rockets landed in tandem on adjacent landing pads in Florida, an absolutely epic feat of engineering. Followed by a framed image of the first Mars landing; it was astonishing for Isaac to think only robots inhabited the planet for so long.

It was time for Isaac to help push the boundaries of humanity and provide new images from outside the solar system for people back on Earth to decorate their walls with.

Isaac thought he had prepared himself for this day. Regardless, he couldn't foresee how the final conversation with his girlfriend would go. He had always had this life goal in mind, so she must have foreseen this day coming as well. He knew not to marry and have kids as it would make this decision more problematic and nothing could deter him from this mission. It had been a rollercoaster over the past few months and the real ride had yet to begin.

The smell of bacon filled his nostrils when he neared the kitchen. How sweet, she graced him with a final home-cooked meal on his last day here on Earth before he only had access to his limited menu on the spaceship. She wanted him to reminisce on his humble beginnings and of his path to making his first billion dollars. The days when he followed all the money-saving advice about making his own coffee at home and eating ramen instead of eating out and all that other nonsense before having anything money could afford. She'd finally accepted his choice to adventure out into the vast unknown to ensure the survival of their species.

To his surprise, the kitchen was empty. Only an "All Day Breakfast" candle lit the middle of the kitchen counter. Candle technology had made progress in the last fifty years. All houses built in the previous century had a built-in scent release to replicate this smell; lighting a candle was an elaborate gesture. Isaac was going to miss this modern farmhouse design in his kitchen. As he approached disappointingly to blow the candle out, a large book laid behind it. It appeared to be a handmade scrapbook covered in glitter titled "My Favorite Memories of Us." Taking the effort to print something out these days was profound. He wasn't always the most emotionally available person, but he would have much rather looked through it together; however, it might be too much to bear and everyone coped with grief in different ways.

Isaac opened the first page of the handmade scrapbook and read the bold letters.

"This page was intentionally left blank."

That was odd, he thought, that was something you'd usually see in an old school educational textbook. He kept flipping.

"This page was intentionally left blank."

"This page was intentionally left blank."

He saw what was going on here. She'd always had a way with words. Maybe it was because he gave most of his remaining money away to charity and not to her, so she could selfishly do who knows what with it. Isaac left her the house, wasn't that enough? He left her the house, which she obviously wouldn't be able to afford maintaining; at least she could sell it for a decent amount and keep herself afloat for a while.

Speaking of floating, Isaac received the alarm that his prescheduled rideshare was almost there to take him to the launch site. He could schedule another one, but he panicked; he had always felt it was rude to make another group of passengers wait for him just to not ride along with them. Isaac rushed back upstairs to throw some clothes on. He would only need these until he got to the Tarax headquarters as they had his clothes and space suit all ready for him there. His wrinkled khaki pants and "Occupy Mars" T-shirt were not what anyone expected a former CEO and soon-to-be former person of their solar system to be wearing. He made a mess, bumping into every piece of furniture on the way out as he frantically emerged from the front door just in time for his vehicle to pull up.

Two other passengers sat inside when he opened the door and took a seat. Only people who were contributing to society, doctors and politicians, or those who were essential to the infrastructure of the city, utility workers and firefighters, could have their own personal vehicles these days. That life was behind Isaac at this point.

The two other passengers were in a heated discussion about which country was going to win the American football match that night. Isaac vaguely knew who was favored to win. The USA was no longer dominant in the sport. He had always thought of it as a barbaric sport even after they had figured out how to avoid all concussions except for the ultrarare cases. As the argument continued, one of the passenger's confidence visibly wavered halfway through the ride and her gaze drifted to the rest of the world outside of the argument.

She finally looked at her phone and back, then at Isaac a few times and said, "I know you. You're Isaac. I used to work for your company. I had only seen your face in emails before and you are not looking like your professional portraits today."

"Thanks," Isaac replied. "I was in a bit of a hurry to head down to the launch site."

"Launch site? Where are you heading? Mars?"

Mostly, only rich people ever left the planet. The majority of folks took a peaceful balloon ride to view the Earth in the stratosphere from thirty thousand meters above the surface. More exclusively, the better-off took small vacations in the Belvedere Space Hotel, the ultimate escape, that orbited the Earth where the ISS used to conduct research. Only the super wealthy and the lucky scientists at the top of their fields took the trip out to Mars.

"No Mars for me, I'm trying to go much further. Somewhere where no one will recognize me on the streets. There won't even be streets where I'm heading."

The rideshare couldn't have dropped him off soon enough at the giant monolith of a building that was Tarax Corporation. If there was any building that wouldn't make you miss Earth, it was this ugly thing. The well-maintained shrubbery in front of the building was pleasant since there weren't many designated green areas in town anymore.

Isaac walked up to the headquarters' large doors and scanned his badge which granted him access to the most secure areas of the building; it was great being a mission commander. To Isaac's surprise, the keypad flashed red, and it released a jarring alarm. Isaac stared at the keypad with perplexity. He scanned again with the same results. This day was starting off great. He saw his favorite receptionist Pam inside and she rushed over to the door and awkwardly apologized for the confusion.

Isaac left the elevator and approached Brian Valenti's CEO suite on the twenty-third floor as he had many times before, though this would be his last.

Large snake plants lined the hallway, guiding him to the giant office that you would expect a CEO of a space travel company to have. Devil's ivy plants scattered around the room that wound up bookshelves and through the rafters. The large, impressive desk ahead of him was filled with different plants: philodendron, fiddle-leaf fig, ZZ plants, and every type of succulent plant you didn't know existed. It was almost as though the CEO of this company was trying to make Isaac miss everything beautiful that planet Earth had to offer right before he abandoned it.

"Quite a thought that the next words you'll hear from Earth could be from my grandchild, or even your own great nephews or nieces if you're leaving any behind," said Brian Valenti, who sat behind his large Tarax Corporation CEO desk.

"Can we talk about my badge access before we get all sentimental?" Isaac sarcastically replied as he scooted out a chair in front of Brian's desk and sat down.

"Ah, we must not have reset your badge deactivation date after the weather delay from your first launch window. Sorry about that."

"This is quite an opportunity you have created here for all of us. I'll be sure to leave a five-star review before we're on our way to Proxima Centauri." Isaac winked. "The badge access issue might have me reconsider that rating, though."

"That's great to hear. Our ratings are astounding. I'm not sure if it's the great customer service we provide here on Earth or if it's the fact that we won't be able to receive a follow-up review until our customers reach their first solar system, a minimum of ninety-two years."

"Most likely the ninety-two-year thing."

"Are you worried we will discover the physics required to create a warp drive and beat you to one of your stops along the way?"

Isaac wondered if that was a question he always asked commanders as they were about to leave the planet. It was like he was trying to convince Isaac that they would invent a more efficient technology in the near future and talk him out of his trip at the last moment.

"You and I both know that isn't going to happen with our United States political two-party government system stagnating any process we plan on making on that front."

"Very smart people are working on it."

"And they have been for hundreds of years. If someone greets me at one of my stops, I'll be glad to hear I told you so. It's best for the survival of humans for us to not plan on that."

They stood up and walked along the observation deck located outside of Brian's office. A long wraparound balcony above where the lift-off procession would take place. Everyone below them knew that their fearless leader was observing, and it would only increase their commitment to the mission. The separation high overhead maintained the larger-than-life status that Isaac had spent years cultivating. He was back at his throne, looking down at the peasants of his former company.

"These people seem like they would follow you on a mission straight into the sun if you asked them politely. I've never seen anything like it," Brian said with a concerned intonation.

"It's easy, just send out a few viral social media posts a week about cats and whatnot and people think you're one of them. I give a lot of credit to social media for keeping the minds of the masses distracted and under my influence."

"I'll never understand. You have to be careful with this cultlike following, though. Having a crew that will keep you in check can completely change the outcome of this entire mission."

"You must get asked this question a lot. Why don't you jump ship on one of the many missions that take off using your services?"

It was always encouraging when the CEO of a company believed in their product and used it, Isaac thought. This wasn't an option here.

"I've already accomplished enough on this giant blue marble of ours floating through space. It's time for me to provide the opportunity to those that still have more time left in their lives to make a difference. That's enough for me."

"You must not have any faith that any of these missions will be successful."

"Who knows, maybe one of my children or someone else further down the line will join you out there."

"Yeah, yeah. No faith. In it to make a quick buck."

"What is it with you billionaire types that feel the need to lead an expedition like this? Why not enjoy your money here?"

"All CEOs are psychopaths; our personality doesn't allow us to sit back and not explore the next frontier. Except for you, I can't figure you out."

"I haven't heard anyone say that about you either. I'm

sure you'll take care of your crew as well as you've taken care of your employees and customers over the years." Brian smirked, knowing Isaac's former company scheduled a union vote for the next morning.

Isaac had an uncanny way of maintaining total control over management while making it seem like everyone else had a say in anything that went on over the years. The illusion faded after giving up control of the company to a much less charismatic CEO. Isaac didn't think there was a need for unions since plenty of laws had passed to prevent mistreatment of the workers who held jobs that were unfulfilled by robots. Union participation was like an unnecessary cult following.

"You've made the specific arrangements," Isaac signaled air quotes with his hands, "that I asked to be included in the ship, correct?"

"Of course, remember those five-star ratings I was telling you about? I just wish I would be alive for another ninety-two years so I could see your first message when you wake up."

"Ninety-two years? I thought it would take eighty-eight years to travel to Proxima Centauri?"

"Yes, four point two light years away, just like how it can take twelve minutes for a message to get to Mars from Earth. We'll have to send your welcome message off earlier, so you'll have a nice update from us as soon as you wake up. We won't receive your response until nine years after we send your first update. Hopefully, things will be in better shape here."

"It's been a long day already. I could really go for an

eighty-eight-year nap right about now."

"Well, do I have some good news for you!"

Looking down at the Countdown to Launch ceremony reminded Isaac of the crew selection process, like an augmented reality video game character selection screen. Virtual reality gaming had gotten to where many people could not tell the difference between it and the real world. He wasn't sure if it was reality or a simulated universe. Would he pick the druid, the warrior, the cleric, the mage, or the priest? Each launch to date saw a perfectly rounded team of the perfect combination of experts to ensure mission success. A perfect balance of the stats listed for each crew member as if they were just a pawn in this interstellar adventure: Agility, Intuition, Intelligence, Adaptability, Emotional Well-Being, and Physical Condition.

The resources had been becoming more and more scarce as the launches continued and Isaac didn't have the luxury of a large pool of candidates. It was time for Isaac to go meet his carefully selected crew for the prelaunch festivities.

The procession path featured a wide, red carpet to give the crew celebrity status in the eyes of the crowds that lined the path leading up to the spacecraft. There was enough of a buffer on either side of the path, with physical barriers in place, to separate them from the masses in order to keep the crew sequestered from possible contamination. The five hundred civilians that signed up to hitch a ride along were all required to attend the ceremony; Tarax found there was a much lower rate of last-minute back-outs after seeing their confident crew glorified on launch day. There were a lot more people lining the procession than the five hundred that signed up. *Are there this many fans of what Tarax is doing?* Maybe they were all paid to attend to increase the allure of space travel.

They couldn't have asked for a more perfect day. It was twenty-two degrees Celsius and not a cloud in the sky, so there shouldn't be another launch scrub today. Isaac walked in front of the crew accompanying him on his ship with the other five crew members in tow, six meters behind them. Isaac kept ahead of his crew and didn't engage with them; however, he paid attention to the surrounding conversations. His engineer, Brad O'Brien, and Isaac's computer scientist, Justine Wong, were to his right. Usha Singh, his psychologist, and Tinah Igwilo, the planetologist, were with him on his left.

Brad was tall with a chiseled jawline and an athletic build, similar to Isaac's, that one would expect to be covered by a professional sports jersey. Justine's short haircut accentuated her defined features; though she was on the shorter side, she looked like his female fitness enthusiast equivalent.

"I can't believe all these people have signed up for this journey. They will all remain in suspended animation for the entire trip with no control over whether they live or die." Justine said awestruck, looking out at the sea of exuberant onlookers. "How are they just okay with placing their destiny in our hands?"

"They have probably seen and experienced my engineering prowess and mechanical work here on Earth. They must have complete confidence and would probably even pay for the opportunity to follow me into the stars," Brad said as he strolled along, soaking in the attention as if the entire audience had come specifically to see him.

"If only they really knew the true you instead of the image created by Isaac and Tarax then I'm sure you couldn't pay them enough money to occupy the same ship as you."

"I really think you're starting to like me. We'll have to get started immediately on the repopulating process as soon as we make it to our new home."

"Gross, I knew I should have left during a previous mission that left the Earth." Justine sighed, "The opportunity to join Isaac slightly outweighs the fact that I have to spend the rest of my life building a new society with you in it."

"I've spent so much time working with computers, you can bet I know how to turn things on," Brad said and winked awkwardly.

"I've heard every bad computer science pickup line there is in grad school, you're not helping your case."

"We have at least a few centuries together before we're home, I'm sure I'll break you down at some point."

Isaac would have to keep his eye on Brad. He had all the technical traits a commander would want when faced with the many potential dangers that came along with interstellar travel; Brad's personality was another issue. Isaac would have to keep him in line and rely on his psychologist to deescalate any conflicts that may arise due to his bravado.

Tinah was a tall individual with longer black hair and

a commanding presence that demanded the attention of anyone around her. Usha was the complete opposite with a calm demeanor that made anyone feel at home around her. Isaac overheard a little of the conversation going on to his left. He wasn't the best at multitasking, though.

"Can you believe these people came out to see us?" Tinah said, off-put by the crowd.

"It's a pretty strange phenomenon. I just keep telling myself they're all here for Isaac and the dream Tarax has envisioned," Usha said. Their psychologist always had a motherly, comforting tone whenever she spoke.

"I know I'm good at what I do. Still, I've never had crowds of people come to cheer me on outside of my laboratory."

"Usually, it is just me and a client engaged in conversation with my line of work. Sometimes there's a family session or couples therapy, never this. I've done a few talks in large lecture halls. You get used to it."

"I'll get used to it today just in time to be lucky enough to share cramped quarters with my four favorite people for an indeterminate amount of time, perfect!"

"Half of these people will be dead when we reach our first destination, so picture them dead. Or you can picture them in their underwear like normal people do, I guess. Whichever you prefer."

They approached the stage, nearing the launch site. It was important for them to provide their last interviews to instill more confidence in their passengers. The stage was massive, with plenty of room for advertising all the companies that contributed to Tarax; space travel wasn't cheap. The crew approached their respective oak lecterns, making them scholarly, as their last known image on Earth before they almost certainly would never return. Their interviewers, small in stature, were exposed in chairs at the other end of the stage, frangible in the presence of the distinguished crew. This ceremony had taken place time and time again as each new mission prepared to take off. The exact movements, the prepared statements, the pageantry. It was meant to duplicate religious ceremonies.

Sit, stand, sit, kneel, sit. Each step meant to indoctrinate the masses into a blind following, which was a tried-and-true routine.

Once all the theatrics Tarax put them through finished, they descended the stairs of the stage and jumped into the electric vehicles to head to the launch site. It was a quiet ride over as the reality of the situation sank in with everyone. This was the last moment to back out.

Approaching the enormous rocket, they stared in awe, mouths agape at the utter size of the machine in front of them. They were basically about to blast off on top of a fifteen-story building loaded to the brim with highly combustible rocket fuel. The elevator ride up filled with more enthusiasm as everyone came to terms with what was about to happen and reality set in as they strapped into their seats.

It would only take eight minutes for their rocket to reach orbit. Nothing could prepare Isaac for the rumble and ferocity of reaching the escape velocity of eleven point two kilometers per second to leave the atmosphere.

Isaac's best ten-kilometer time running on Earth was just under an hour and they would travel that distance within a second to overcome Earth's gravitational pull. Isaac tried to think about the personnel of the other crew as he was being smashed against the back of his seat while they made their accent toward the final frontier.

Isaac was jealous of the other commander, Victoria Bowers, who had experience that no one else in either of the ships had; she had been to space before. Victoria had spent a five-hundred-day cycle on Mars as an environmental scientist researching technologies that would improve population sustainability and would be extremely valuable once they made it to their destination. Isaac wished Victoria was on his ship. However, they would need a powerful leader to take over in case something was to happen to him or his ship. Isaac was mostly jealous of the fact that she had been in this hot seat before and knew what to expect during the launch.

The rapid acceleration ended just as abruptly as it had started, causing the stuffed animal frog zero-gravity indicator to fly across his face, which indicated they made it into orbit.

Chapter Two

Victoria
(Earth: Year 2302)

"I've spent my entire life thinking that I'm the only person fit for the job of solving every issue that has been placed in front of me, this is different."

-The Hypersleep Chronicles

Space tourism had given many affluent individuals the opportunity to feel the overview effect and Victoria couldn't help from feeling the same way as she saw the Earth from this altitude again. Seeing her fragile planet from the vantage point of what some people would consider the heavens made Victoria feel like Earth might have been heaven all along. None of the petty office disputes or quarrels between family or friends mattered with this view.

There was only one place on the planet where she could still see an international border at night between two countries with the naked eye: North Korea and South Korea. Victoria had always dreamed of a unified Korean country, but that dream had never come to fruition. This unwavering situation was a stark and disheartening reminder that some things may never change and they must always seek to improve their situation elsewhere in the galaxy.

Many dangers occurred in interstellar space, especially when the crew would be in a deep slumber for decades and sometimes even centuries at a time. It was best to spread out the risk across two ships in case either succumbed to the various perils awaiting them. It was finally time to rendezvous with the two glorious chariots that would sweep them away into the vast unknown. Isaac's ship, the Arbitrary Algorithm, and its companion, the Recursive Singularity, were in a steady free fall toward Earth, waiting for the two commanders to steer the vessels toward adventure.

Isaac was ultimately the commander of both ships. When something would happen to him, then the commander of the Recursive Singularity, Victoria, would take over. There was a chain of command that went on after Victoria. She hoped nothing would turn that scenario into a reality, but Victoria secretly wanted to be the main commander of this mission. She had been playing second fiddle her entire life ever since she was snubbed for first chair in her high school orchestra by that conniving Christina Callahan.

Victoria's crew had an engineer, Stephanie Williams, who had an impressive resume and was much less of a hothead than the other engineer, Brad. There was a psychologist, James Solkowitz, who was necessary for any high-stress and potentially long-range mission in space. Amy Pierce was on their ship for any biology needs. She would help in determining the level of the intelligence of a species if they were to run into complex life on another planet. Last, Raul Suarez rounded out the group as their physician. They shouldn't run into any medical emergencies on the way, but Raul would be invaluable once they land.

It was comforting having such a competent crew traveling alongside Victoria and she wondered who had the better teammates on their ship, her or Isaac. Regardless, one team one dream. Teamwork makes the dream work.

The spacecrafts were sectioned off into two main areas. There was one large section where their five hundred stowaway passengers would be staying. A stationary section where they would remain in cryo-sleep for the entire trip. There was no need for gravity as their chambers would keep them in pristine condition until they arrived at their new home. Rows and rows of chambers like a mausoleum storing their great, great relatives. Except these folks would eventually rise from the dead. Hopefully.

The crew section was a little less grim. A rotating section around their esteemed stowaway passengers simulated gravity with centrifugal force to ensure their bodies wouldn't deteriorate while they put in the work to find their new paradise. It would take the crews three days to regain their bearings after their long sleep in between star systems and a couple more days to decide if they stayed or moved on. They would need to stick to this strict schedule to remain in contact with Tarax Corporation on Earth.

The main control center was where they would be most of the time conducting research. The dining hall had one decent-sized table for five, which featured a small kitchen station that would make any corporate office kitchen station on Earth not jealous. There was the hibernation room, where their sleep chambers would allow them to travel between the stars within one human lifetime. A respectable gymnasium equipped with a treadmill, rowing machine, bench, and a squat rack. Last, there were five rooms that would give everyone some privacy and most likely much-needed space away from each other while orbiting different planets and conducting research.

It took about eighteen hours after the launch to match orbits with the Arbitrary Algorithm and the Recursive Singularity to seal up with the airlock and climb aboard. It felt like they were checking into a hotel for the first time, walking around, opening every door and cabinet, and saying things like “this is nice.” There were exact replicas of every room they had explored on Earth, although, nothing was quite like the real thing.

Isaac’s voice came over their ship’s intercom system, “This is Isaac with the Arbitrary Algorithm, checking communications with the Recursive Singularity, over.”

“This is Victoria with the Recursive Singularity, confirming communications, loud and clear.”

“Once our passengers are all loaded and frozen, we will set course for Proxima Centauri.”

"Confirmed, we'll see you on the other side."

As the excitement settled down after exploring every inch of the ship, it was time for the crew to find their way into their sleep chambers. They had all experienced short-term cryo-sleep on Earth when they were training for the mission. However, there were still questions about the effects of experiencing multiple decades in hibernation. They were about to find out what would happen when a group of people placed themselves into cryo-sleep for multiple decades in a spacecraft cruising through space at 5 percent of the speed of light. The chamber slowly closed on Victoria and she drifted into a deep sleep.

Victoria woke up in a daze, not recognizing her surroundings. She couldn't move most of her body including her neck which prevented her from noticing anything else in the room. This really added to her confusion. She gazed at a control panel directly in front of her that stretched two meters wide, with buttons and bright lights.

The ship's voice filled the room with an inquisition. "What is your name?"

She was completely dumbfounded. Looking around the room was a tough task as it was and now there was this omnipotent voice asking a tough question.

"I'm not sure," Victoria replied.

"Take the green pill on the table to your right, your brain needs more time to adjust after your long sleep."

Her long sleep? There was an odd familiarity with the situation. She couldn't put her finger on it. Waking up in a mysterious control room, in what appeared to be space, with a robotic voice telling her to take a strange pill. What could go wrong? She complied with her new robot friend. She took the green pill and drifted back into a slumber.

Victoria woke up again to the same robotic voice that had introduced itself the day before.

"What is your name?" the robot asked.

Annoyed by the repetition of the questions, Victoria replied, "Victoria, how many times are you going to ask me that?"

"Good, we're making some progress."

Victoria was finally able to move her neck and limbs with relative ease; there were four other tanks in the room that contained the bodies of people unrecognizable to her. The windows were dark, but there appeared to be a planet floating off in the distance that resembled Earth.

"Who are these other people?"

"That's not important at the moment. Do you know why you're here?"

"I'm assuming it's just not to make friends with strange robots that tell me to ingest random things?"

"It's not. I am your ship's AI. Eighty-eight years ago, you left everything behind and co-command a space mission to help lead a crew of ten, along with five hundred others in suspended animation, to find another world to live on instead of relying on Earth as the only planet for humans to exist on. You have reached your first stop on this mission and have woken up a few days before the rest of your crew in order to have a jump start on the wake-up routine so you can assist in their first adjustments in space."

That did sound like something she would do.

"When am I going to remember all of this? Are we going to have this conversation again, or will it ever get easier?"

"Unfortunately, for me, we will most likely go through this process repeatedly. It will feel like the first time for you each time. Time for another green pill and you should be mostly back to normal the next time you wake up."

"Well, I did wake up after the first pill. I guess I can trust you again."

She reluctantly complied, and everything around her faded into darkness.

The darkness returned to light as her beautiful girlfriend, Gigi, gently shook her awake to reveal a large dome-shaped shelter where they resided. A baby cried in the distance and the sun had just started to rise and illuminate the frosted glass windows of the rounded structure.

Victoria sat up and tried to figure out what was going on.

"Where am I?" Victoria asked.

"Your chamber must have malfunctioned, and the crew had to help you out of the ship. You've been steady in and out of it ever since we landed," Gigi answered.

"We landed? What do you mean?"

"We have made it to our new home. They weren't able to unfreeze you on the ship, so, they ended up having to complete the entire mission without you. Without your help, they were able to find the perfect new home for us."

Victoria looked around in total disbelief.

"You stayed on Earth. How did you get here?" Victoria inquired.

"I wanted to keep it a secret, but I was stowed away, frozen on your ship in the passenger section the entire time. I couldn't bear the thought of being with anyone besides you, so I decided to see if there was anyone that would back out at the last moment and pulled some strings to be at the front of the standby line."

Victoria didn't know what to say as she continued to just stare at her girlfriend, trying to comprehend everything that was happening.

Gigi backed away toward a small object that looked like a crib.

"Why aren't you saying anything? Aren't you excited we get to spend the rest of our new lives together?"

Victoria was stunned, her mind blank, as fear twisted firmly within her. She couldn't envision what horrors lay from within this crib.

"Plus, the real surprise." Gigi lowered her arms into the crib and lifted a crying baby. "The intrauterine insemination was successful. I was pregnant before we left Earth!"

Victoria's jaw rested on the floor. She was always against having kids with Gigi, and especially not like this.

Gigi walked the baby over to her and placed the small baby girl in her arms. The baby stared at her adoringly, then spoke, "Victoria, Victoria, wake up, Victoria."

Victoria woke up from the dream in a cold sweat to more monotonous questions from her robot buddy and it all came back to her. Just a dream. Dodged a bullet there.

It was finally time for some of Victoria's questions to be answered.

"So, what can I call you?" Victoria asked.

"My name is Karina. You can change my name if you prefer."

"Karina it is. Who are my human friends here?"

They were all vaguely familiar. Similar to guessing the faces of acquaintances from a twenty-year high school reunion. Except she wasn't at the high school reunion to give her the context clues of where she knew them from. Just random faces that looked oddly like people she had once known in her distant past.

"This is your carefully selected crew you brought with you from Earth. Your engineer, Stephanie. Your psychologist, James. Your biologist, Amy."

"Wait, wait. Let me guess, that's Raul?" She gestured at the last tank.

"Yes. Your physician."

"How did I know that?"

"By the end of day three, you should have most of the puzzle put together."

"That's fantastic news. Is it alright if I get out of this tank and explore the ship?"

"Sure. After all, it is your ship, co-commander."

Victoria used most of her strength to lift herself out of the chamber that she'd been in for eighty-eight years and perused the other tanks. Her mind was foggy, and her muscles weren't awake yet. Although Stephanie and Raul were the farthest away from each other, she remembered a strange bond between them. Maybe they were related? She thought James a trustworthy person. Someone who would probably get approached by random strangers that would confide their deepest and darkest secrets to him without even knowing who he was. Amy looked like someone who would lead a crew like this. She really hoped she would get to meet them soon, or perhaps reunite with them?

She left the room and stumbled down the hall and found a dining hall first. Victoria raided all the cabinets aimlessly, like it was a different floor's kitchenette at an office she just started working at. She was trying to find some coffee or tea or anything with caffeine in it. There was a treasure trove of coffee in the upper right cabinet. Quite a selection too. She fixed herself a little Sumatra blend. Whoever had picked the coffee possessed great taste. Perhaps it was her?

Victoria was still having trouble remembering everything. With her caffeine kick, she gazed out of the windows, which offered an incredible view of a planet and another ship floating nearby at a comfortable distance away. Maybe she could ask Karina what's up with that other ship? In hindsight, she could have just asked her where the coffee was, too.

"Karina, what's going on with that other ship? Can I talk to it?"

"Sure, at any time. Just ask me to open communications with the Arbitrary Algorithm."

"Arbitrary Algorithm? What idiot picked that name?"

"The main commander of this expedition, Isaac."

"Isaac," Victoria said inquisitively. The name tickled her brain, but no matter how hard she thought about it, a face did not accompany the name. "I guess I shouldn't call the main commander an idiot. Karina, open communications with the Arbitrary Algorithm."

"You're connected."

"Hello, Isaac, with the Arbitrary Algorithm. This is Victoria with ..." she didn't even know the name of her ship, "the other ship you've probably noticed floating near you. Can you hear me?"

"Hello, this is Isaac with the Arbitrary Algorithm, apparently. Did you find the coffee over there?"

"Upper right cabinet over here, probably the same on your ship. I'm still trying to figure out everything that is going on. I just wanted to check your status over there."

"Same status over here. I'll keep you posted."

"Right back at you."

Victoria spent the rest of the day exploring the ship and even got a decent workout at the gymnasium to help get her body and mind activated. Exhaustion weighed on her. She still wasn't herself like back on Earth. Victoria located the private quarters titled with her name and relaxed into bed. Sleep came to her easily.

Finally feeling like herself, Victoria monitored the slow progress of the crew to get their wits about them after leaving suspended animation. She woke them up one by one to make scrupulous observations of how they all adjusted to their new environment. *It's a much more pleasant experience being on this side of the conversation*, she thought. Victoria had much more training than the others, but she was still anxious to run through the procedures with the crew and to move on to the first real potential solar system after this practice run. There were months of preparation on Earth, and every procedure had been spelled out explicitly. However, nothing can prepare you for the real thing. The crew all gathered in the command center.

"The first step is to check for updates from Earth. Each time we wake up, tens or hundreds of years will have passed since we have last heard from back home and a lot can change," Victoria explained.

"Earth has evolved eighty-eight years in this message since we've been there?" asked Amy.

"Well, almost eighty-four years. You have to remember that any messages take four point two five years to get here, so they sent the signal out years before we even got here," Victoria answered.

"That's encouraging to hear that the Earth has lasted at least eighty-four more years. That's much longer than I was expecting," Raul said. He had a similar outlook that Victoria had about Earth's future. Regardless, she didn't want to cultivate any negativity here.

"Humans could have gone extinct anytime in the last four point two five years?" Amy asked as she shifted her weight in her chair and scooted back a little. "And we would have no idea about it?"

"That's physics, and depending on how long we're here and how long it takes to get to our next stop, we won't hear about their status for at least another century."

Victoria explained the concept like it was perfectly normal, even though the gravity of their situation was taking hold of her.

"That's pretty dark stuff," Raul said as he raised his eyebrows and smiled in a slightly sadistic way.

"One hundred seventy-six years will have passed by on Earth if we turned around and headed straight back today," noted Stephanie.

A long silence ensued, as it seemed like the crew started to truly realize the irreversibility of the decision to follow their leaders into the depths of their seemingly endless universe. Everyone they had loved, made friends and acquaintances with, or would even recognize on Earth, would have long passed away even if they would turn around and head back at this point. This thought weighed heavily on everyone. Victoria needed to interrupt this somber situation.

"Let's see what has happened on Earth since we have left, Karina," Victoria said.

The recording played on the command center screen:

"Welcome to your first stop on your multigenerational space journey! The year is 2386. Space travel is still a booming industry in the private sector, as it has been since 2302 when your crew departed. There have been waves of crews leaving the Earth over the years as we experience the ebbs and flows of accumulating willing and qualified people to start the journey.

"Terraforming efforts on Mars continue to move at a glacial pace but are steadily moving forward. Eventually, red will rise. All major nations' bases on Mars are expanding and we are worried that they will begin encroaching on each other's land. Hopefully, this won't cause the same sort of territorial disputes that we have experienced on Earth over the centuries. Our base on Luna continues to thrive, and we will soon have bases on Ceres and Ganymede. Nothing exciting on the Earth front, we just continue to buzz right along. We will send everyone updates via private files from their friends and relatives from Earth. I'm sure there will be a lot to digest.

"To this day, we still have not received communications from any crews that have left the Earth due to the time it takes for messages to be received from our closest neighboring star in the galaxy. I'm sure there is data on the way from other crews that left the Earth before you. Please send us your research before you head out to your next location.

"Thanks for choosing Tarax Corporation for your space travel needs!"

That was the rosy picture. Victoria wondered how much of that was accurate and how much was embellished to make it seem like they made the right decision to leave Earth. There wasn't any way to tell, as their only communication with Earth was through Tarax.

The crew ran through the rest of the procedures and everyone was finally back in their quarters for the night, reading through their personal updates. This was the moment Victoria was dreading since she first signed up for her mission with Tarax. Would she open her private Earth updates? Victoria had long had the view that her bloodline should end with her because of the overall recurring theme of dysfunction in her family line. She was successful in doing so, on Earth at least. Victoria almost considered opting out of the update altogether. She still wanted to at least put off the decision until she was in the situation she was in at this very moment. Her finger hovered over the open button, hesitatingly, and she begrudgingly ended up hitting the delete button. There was most likely a way to recover the files, but she figured it was best to keep everything in the past.

Chapter Three

Tinah
(Arbitrary Algorithm: Year 88)

"Maybe the initial parameters were too strict for a solar system to move to. Maybe the perfect place just isn't out there."

-The Hypersleep Chronicles

Tinah and the crew of the Arbitrary Algorithm had just listened to the first message from Earth and were moving along to their second procedure.

"New friend, Karina," Tinah said. She thought it was so nice having a new friend to boss around instead of only taking orders from Isaac. "Bring up the solar system stats for our first stop."

The screen in the command center displayed the data:

Proxima Centauri
Distance (Light Years from Earth): 4.25
Apparent Magnitude: 11.13
Stellar Classification: M6V

Planets of Interest:

Proxima Centauri b
Mass: 1.3
Radius: 1.08
Period (Days): 11.2

Proxima Centauri c
Mass: 7
Radius: 2.2
Period (Days): 1,928

Isaac was examining the data and finally said, "It's great to see all of our sensors and imagery are working as expected. Tinah, as our resident planetologist, would you be able to give us an overview of what we are seeing here?"

These statistics were familiar to everyone, but this was one of Isaac's least favorite topics when going through their training back on Earth. Isaac was a leader first and didn't like to encumber himself with the details some-times. Describing them to the crew would be a simple task, even for Isaac, but he probably figured it would be nice to include Tinah and give her a chance to shine. Delegating tasks was his specialty on Earth and the thing which allowed him to rise to the top, so he was most likely to keep that going throughout the galaxy.

"I would love to," Tinah said and then cleared her throat. "Proxima Centauri is four point two five light years from Earth and is in the top two on a list of stars closest to our home originating planet."

Usha had a questioning gaze and finally asked, "So it's second after our beloved Sol?"

"That's correct, Sol is about eight light minutes away from Earth. The sun could burn out and the people of Earth wouldn't know it for eight whole minutes. Our last planet in the solar system, Neptune, which sits an average of thirty AU away from Sol, wouldn't know the sun burned out for four hours."

"What's an AU?" Usha asked.

"Astronomical units, the mean distance from the center of Earth to the center of its star, Sol. From our perspective, if we were to grab a telescope and look back at Earth, we would see it as it existed four point two five years ago. And the same would go for an Earth observer looking directly at us. We would still be far from our destination."

"That's pretty zany," Brad added.

"Apparent magnitude is the brightness of a celestial body, as observed on Earth. Proxima Centauri's apparent magnitude to the Earth is eleven point one three, and this number is decreased by a star's brightness and increased as the distance increases from Earth. This star is pretty close to the Earth and isn't bright compared to other stars."

"Not so bright," Justine interjected, "that's something Brad and this star have in common."

Everyone laughed besides their engineer, Brad, and the ship's AI, Karina, of course.

Tinah continued, "Proxima Centauri is spectral type M, which is the most common in our cosmic neighborhood. The '6V' indicates it is a run-of-the-mill red dwarf star on the low-mass end of an M-type star with a red-yellow color. Planet mass here is measured as compared to Earth. We can see that Proxima b has a little more mass than Earth and Proxima c has a much larger mass than the planet we have vacated. Proxima c is about half the mass of Uranus. Brad, don't even start."

"I didn't say anything," Brad said, as he smirked and looked around the room with delight.

"Get it out of your system. Proxima b has a slightly bigger radius than Earth, which means its greater mass makes it a little denser than Earth," said Tinah.

"You're like this planet too," Justine mentioned as she pointed at Brad. "Dense, you get it? You'll get it, eventually."

Brad groaned. Everyone else was amused. Karina was probably amused.

"Anyway," Tinah continued. "Proxima c has a little more than double the radius of the Earth with seven times the mass which some would classify it as a Super Earth. The intense gravity on this Proxima c would make it very difficult to leave the ground if you were to jump on the surface. This would make it tough to live with our human bodies without the help of some sort of modifications or an exoskeleton. Proxima b is whizzing around Proxima Centauri and completes a full revolution every eleven point two standard Earth days. This would mean a person who has lived for thirty Earth years would have experienced about nine hundred eighty trips around Proxima Centauri if they lived here. In contrast, Proxima c completes one trip around its host star every one thousand nine hundred twenty-eight Earth days. So, how many trips around Proxima Centauri would thirty Earth years allow you? Anyone? Anyone?"

"Five point six eight three two two nine two …" Karina replied.

"That's not even fair," said Usha.

That Karina was a sassy one, Tinah wondered if there was a way to adjust her sassiness setting up or down, though she liked her current level of sassiness for now.

After a brief silence, Isaac said, "There isn't a lot of research to do here as we know we will not be settling down in this system, we just wanted to get a dry run in to see how things would work before we make it somewhere that was of potential value. I'll give everyone the evening off to review their personal updates from Earth so they can laugh or cry or however they need to react and process eighty-four years of events."

Tinah caught Isaac in the weight room later that day as he worked out on the rowing machine; she could never get into a rhythm on those things. She absolutely hated it when people talked to her at the gym, but this was a good opportunity to get in a good word with the commander while the endorphins were flowing. She walked over to the treadmill and scanned the screen as if she had never used one before, hoping Isaac would pause his workout to engage her in conversation instead of her interrupting him.

Isaac slowly returned the handlebar back toward the rowing machine and removed the straps from his shoes. Turning his head to Tinah, he said, "Tinah, thanks for all the fun facts about our current location back in the command center. This is exactly why I wanted you on my ship. You seemed a little troubled by the events of the day though."

Tinah turned to Isaac in surprise like she hadn't seen him there and draped her arm over the handlebar of the treadmill closest to the rowing machine. "Dreaming about this day and actually experiencing it are two different things, I suppose," Tinah said and shrugged as she answered. She had never guessed this situation would make her long for Earth as much as it did and especially didn't realize how much others could read that feeling from her expressions.

"Would you say you are a more risk-averse individual?"

"My entire life has been spent being quite the daredevil. Early on, I was way ahead of any other child as far as motor skills and exploring the world around me. Whether it was riding a bike or rollerblading or hiking, I was always the first to venture out and push the boundaries."

"We are definitely similar in that regard. That's the CEO mindset that propelled me in front of everyone else."

"I spent months of my early days with broken bones, as other kids signed my various casts and tried to become my friend. Everyone wanted to help me limp to my next classroom so they could get out of class early. I wasn't always the smartest, however, I was out there testing the laws of physics and learning the consequences of my actions."

"So, a crash course in physics?" Isaac asked.

"Something like that. This naturally progressed into more adventurous activities like skydiving, spelunking, and even racing cars. As my body told me those things weren't an option anymore, I traveled. My first trip to Iceland showed me just how beautiful this world could be. I'm so glad my friend talked me into that first international trip."

"I guess that sort of explains why you got into geology and whatnot."

"Precisely. The black sand beaches of Reynisfjara, glacier lagoons, waterfalls like Gullfoss, geysers scattered across the land, the Aurora Borealis. I just couldn't get enough of what our beautiful planet had to offer."

Tinah might have stayed on Earth if she had this conversation with Isaac on launch day. That toothpaste had already left the proverbial tube and wasn't going back in. The ominous feeling of regret crept in that she rarely ever experienced in her life until this point. She felt sick even though she hadn't started her dizzying CrossFit routine she had planned.

"Who would ever want to leave a place like that?" Isaac asked.

"Well, I got more daring as the time went on. Leaving the resorts in Cancun and Punta Cana to go on side quests without my friends turned into solo trips halfway across the world to Australia and New Zealand. I was really putting myself into dangerous situations in some not-so-great parts of the world. So, I headed out to the last frontier in space. I felt like my luck was running out on Earth and eventually my precarious behavior would catch up to me. I would much rather die out here in space trying to ensure the survival of humanity than end up in the ground as just another tourist who pushed the boundaries a little too far."

"I'm glad I get to help provide you with the ultimate travel experience. I felt in a pretty similar way that I would regret it if I was buried on the same planet I was born on, and Mars was not much better. I'm excited to seek out the planet we'll have the privilege of being buried on together."

Tinah was the last person to head back to her private quarters after a long, intense workout. She walked in and plopped down on the comfy twin bed that reminded her of freshman year of college. Tinah opened a cabinet drawer beside her bed, a small book laid inside. She was reminded of the time when she was staying in a hotel in Utah and discovered the Book of Mormon inside. Tinah picked the book up and read the title *Philosophiae Naturalis Principia Mathematica*. A book much more appropriate for an interstellar journey.

She grabbed her tablet to review her personal Earth

updates and thought about all the scenarios that could have happened on Earth since they had been there. Did her best friend end up getting married, settling down, and having the two kids she had always dreamed of having? She did. There were photos of them in front of their beautiful house in the suburbs with their adorable white picket fence she had always fawned over. Did her parents live out the rest of their lives and pass on peacefully of old age? Also, a yes. Tinah only had one sister that also didn't plan on having children, so no grandchildren for her parents.

No personal updates from her boyfriend who she had left behind, though she figured this may be the case as they didn't leave things on the best of terms. Only a news article had been sent to her by her sister. She assumed it was about him, "Another Life Lost to the Failing Drug War." She had spent years trying to keep him from the constant relapse of abusing drugs. She wouldn't have felt bad for him if his addiction to painkillers hadn't resulted from a rear-end car accident. He was prescribed a medication that would prove impossible to not rely on, and it eventually consumed him entirely.

Tinah finally ended up choosing a journey that would take her away from it all. Her boyfriend could only help himself at this point and there was no use allowing him to hold her back any longer.

She had spent months and months between the terrible feelings of caring too much and guilt when she had hoped to just find him dead one day. Tinah hoped she wouldn't have to choose between leaving him on her own accord or sticking around to see if he would change. She figured some other woman would swoop in to save him and steer him in the right direction after she had left Earth. She didn't want to see it end like this. Regardless, seeing this article validated her decision to not stick around and witness this misfortune firsthand.

Tinah had always kept herself busy on Earth to prevent her from feeling a consuming rush of sorrow like this. With nowhere else to go and nothing else to keep her occupied, she cried until the eventual exhaustion of weeping forced her to sleep.

Tinah awoke and strolled by the large window near the command center, peering into the endless sea of possibilities the universe offered, impossible to tire of. Seeing the two other ships that accompanied them on their journey always brought her a sense of assurance as they ventured into the great abyss. Sailing off to discover new worlds that would lead to the goal of conquering new land and providing a great wealth of knowledge and opportunity for our motherland. She thought they left Earth with only two ships total, though. One of these other two ships wasn't a part of the original fleet. One of them was much swifter and more maneuverable and heading right toward them.

A boisterous, feminine human voice rang out from the ship's speakers, "Prepare your airlocks to be boarded."

Did Earth send a ship that could catch up to them? She assumed it was possible eventually if they didn't make any stops like their crew had, but Tarax would have told the crew at their first stop at Proxima Centauri if another ship was pursuing them. There's no way it could have caught up with them if they had left after Earth recorded the initial message, unless they developed some new space travel technology. Maybe it was some sort of extra-terrestrial space pirate that wanted to raid their ships. The alien beings could disguise their spacecraft to look like theirs in order to not alert them and prevent them from some sort of countermeasures of aggression. Either way, there wasn't much she could do to prevent this annexation.

The ship matched their velocity and orientation inconceivably that would never be imagined given the technology present when Tinah had left Earth behind. A telescopic gangway emerged from the foreign vessel heading right toward their airlock. The end of the structure transformed and took on a shape matching perfectly with the dimensions of their airlock to create a perfect seal. The crew gathered and grabbed anything that resembled a weapon in preparation for the imminent donnybrook. They headed to the airlock to greet whoever or whatever was about to emerge from the foreign craft.

A hiss of air released as the airlock cycled and the doors slowly parted. To her surprise, the beings on the other side looked just like them and they all let out a sigh of relief. There was a woman in the front with a short haircut and two other larger men standing behind her that looked like her bodyguards. They took a step into their ship like they owned the place.

"Greetings," the woman said in a heartening tone.

"I'm hoping those objects in your hands are gifts you're offering to us and not objects you're planning to bash us over the head with."

"I guess our conversation will decide the fate of these objects," Isaac replied.

"No need to worry. My name is Elizabeth. Elizabeth from Earth. We came to rescue you."

"Rescue us? From what? We were fleeing the Earth!"

"Tarax Corporation has been brought under federal investigation by the governments of Earth on numerous charges for negligence. We are happy that you are still alive. They knew that most of their ships wouldn't make it far past the nearest star system. They figured that they were shielded from liability based on the fact that no one would know about their lies for hundreds, if not thousands of years. Your ship was never intended to last long enough to make it anywhere of actual interest and they were raking in millions based on these lies."

"This can't be true; you're lying to us. How would you be able to meet us out here this fast? Why wouldn't you just send us a message once we got here," Tinah said. The ominous feeling of regret that she felt earlier was about to win the fight and completely consume her.

"Earth has made many advancements as you and your crew sat dormant, drifting through the interstellar medium. The dream of faster than light travel has finally been realized, and we have been sent out to retrieve the few Tarax ships that still survive. We have colonized exoplanets in many star systems that we could have never imagined since the days of the evil Tarax Corporation. We will take you all back to Earth, where you can decide which of our new worlds you would like to build a new life on."

"Our whole trip was for nothing?" Tinah asked.

"Not for nothing, think about all the friends you made along the way."

Tinah's legs trembled and all she could remember was seeing the ceiling as everything faded to black.

Tinah awoke back in her cabin; it was just a dream. The feeling of desolation was still present, even though none of it was real.

The morning commenced with small talk about whichever information everyone was willing to share about their personal files. Isaac divulged his girlfriend did in fact, end up selling their house like he had thought she would. She also ended up blowing all the money on online poker, exactly as he had imagined. Brad didn't have anything exciting to say. Tinah wasn't sure if that was because he hadn't left much behind on Earth or if he was more of a private person who didn't want everyone in his business. He was hard to read. Justine had a fairytale story for everyone she had left behind on Earth. Tinah wondered why she had ever left. Usha was more of a stoic person who closed all her loose ends on Earth. There was a doctor-patient confidentiality she had with all her professional and personal relationships alike.

Tinah told the others about her family she left behind and how her only regret was not giving her parents grandchildren. Her parents were not content with the fish in the aquarium that she had left behind for them to take care of. Tinah didn't mention her boyfriend to the others, as she wanted to keep that chapter of her life closed. She was in a much better place after leaving that toxic relationship behind.

Everyone seemed to accept their situation here, and they were content with the way things turned out in what most likely would have been the rest of their lifespan on Earth. It was time for them all to lie down for their second hibernation on the way to their second solar system.

Chapter Four

Brad
(Arbitrary Algorithm: Year 314)

"No one else would have the willpower and determination to do what I'm doing, and it will pay off in the end."

-The Hypersleep Chronicles

The entire crew waking up at the same time was a little more of a fun experience for everyone involved. They all got to question the ship's AI together and then reluctantly consume the pills that returned them back into a questionably long, additional slumber. They were able to receive the introduction together and slowly confirm everything Karina was telling them by combining the collective pieces of their incomplete memories. It was day four of the wake-up process at their second stop and it was finally time to start the procedures that were established for each actual stop on their journey. First, time for a nice update from Earth.

"Hey Karina, what's been going on with Earth since our last stop?" Isaac asked.

The silence went on for about twenty seconds as everyone slowly met eyes with each other. It was awkward for everyone involved.

"Karina," Brad said as he tilted his head, "the Earth update?"

"There seems to be some sort of error. We have no update from Earth," Karina finally replied.

"You know I love being right all the time, however, I certainly wouldn't enjoy being correct about my decision to leave everyone behind to their inevitable extinction," Isaac said.

"What could have happened?" Usha inquired.

"It would be the year 2616 on Earth. There are a bunch of things that could have happened given this amount of Earth time. This is why I wanted to leave in the first place," Isaac replied.

"Do you think it was some sort of deadly pandemic? Like what we thought was going to happen in 2020?" asked Usha.

"It's possible. Not likely after we had that dress rehearsal. There hasn't been an overreaction to a virus like that since 2020," Isaac replied.

"Aliens," Brad mentioned sarcastically as he held his hands up in front of him. He had always contemplated that a hostile apex predator species would be the way humans went extinct.

"Anything is possible. Maybe a meteor strike. Maybe a super volcano like Yellowstone finally erupted?" Tinah said.

"Could the sun have burned out?" Usha asked. "I saw that in a documentary once."

"The sun had billions of years of life remaining before we departed and we haven't even been traveling for a thousand years," Isaac replied.

After a long silence, Brad interrupted, "Definitely aliens."

Convinced that was the solution to their enigma, Brad's heart raced with terror as he wondered if the aliens could follow their route from Tarax headquarters and seek their spaceship out.

"Well, whatever happened, it only brings additional significance to the importance of our mission. Failure was not an option before and now we potentially have the fate of humanity on our shoulders if no other mission has found a suitable home," Isaac said as he brought an end to the speculation. "Karina, what's the report for our current solar system?"

The screen in the command center displayed the data:

Jacobs-452
Distance (Light Years from Earth): 14.1
Apparent Magnitude: 2.57
Stellar Classification: G2V

Planets of Interest:

Jacobs-452b
Mass: 0.48
Radius: 0.72
Period (Days): 342

Jacobs-452c
Mass: 2.91
Radius: 1.28
Period (Days): 439

Jacobs-452d
Mass: 1.23
Radius: 3.1
Period (Days): 503

"There is a unique planet here outside of the Goldilocks zone almost twice the size of Earth and ten times the mass of Earth. The planet is so massive that the star and the planet orbit each other around a center point outside of the star, kind of like the sun and Jupiter in our home solar system. This carbon rich environment coupled with the immense gravity means this planet is covered in diamonds." Tinah looked at Justine and Usha as she spoke. "This planet is a girl's best friend."

"Brad, if we settled down here, you might have a big enough supply of diamonds for all of your future ex-wives' rings," joked Justine.

"This is quite an interesting star here," Tinah said as she pondered the possibilities. "I'm surprised there is the opportunity for life in this system. It would differ from what we're used to."

"So, you're saying there's a chance?" Brad asked as he was showing his upper teeth and glaring at Tinah. No one understood the reference.

"Unfortunately, there is not a chance for us. Earth's atmosphere is made up of seventy-eight percent nitrogen, twenty-one percent oxygen, point nine percent argon, and the last point one percent is other trace amounts of gasses. We need an atmosphere that consists of at least nineteen point five percent oxygen in order to survive and no more than twenty-three point five percent ideally." Tinah continued to explain, "If the level of oxygen is less than nineteen point five percent, our cells might not receive the oxygen they need to function and could fail. It is survivable under that limit. Although mental functions are impaired, breathing is tougher, and it just wouldn't be a sustainable life. Oxygen over that limit is again livable, but the much-increased risk of fires and explosions and lengthy exposure would certainly cause health risks."

"I'm guessing you are explaining all of this because none of these planets provide this range of oxygen?" asked Brad.

"Look at the big brain on Brad!" Justine exclaimed. Everyone understood that reference and acknowledged her humor.

Brad looked at Isaac with bewilderment and asked, "Why would we even come to this system?"

"There's only so much our telescopes orbiting Earth can tell us, using the transit method, before we head out on these missions." Isaac was defending leaving Earth. "We can get a good idea of what chemicals exist in a planet's atmosphere to give us a best guess of which planets to check out. At the end of the day, we just know where to explore and we need to send our probes out once we get here in order to see exactly what we're working with in an exoplanet's atmosphere."

Usha interrupted to defend Isaac, "We all knew we didn't know exactly what these planets were before we started."

Isaac added, "We need at least one planet to be move-in ready to provide a base, and then we can work on terraforming the other planets once we get our home base established. There isn't anywhere here to get started. I'll send all this information back to Earth and hopefully someone is waiting for our signal to relay to the other ships so they don't stop here."

"Can we swing by that diamond planet and stock up?" Usha asked.

Justine raised her hand and said, "I second that."

"Third," said Tinah.

Another message popped up on the screen in front of them. Brad figured the Earth message just came in later than usual, maybe, because of aliens?

"Greetings, humans. We have been observing your movements and society for decades. We have deciphered your languages, observed your traditions, and learned everything we could about your feeble existence. You have made your planet so easily noticeable in the vastness of space through openly broadcasting your signals in every direction, foolish. Sending explicit photographs of your species on a golden plaque out into space. What was that about? You and your ship are not welcome here. Completely imprudent of you to think that any other extraterrestrial species smart enough to notice you would want to coexist with such an abominable group of creatures. We do not have the technology yet to leave our planet ourselves. As we've watched your approach, we have developed the technology to repulse you from our orbit. You have three Earth days to begin your retreat."

Brad had always wondered if it was more concerning if there were other intelligent life in the universe or if there was no alien life besides themselves. This was a possibility, but never in his wildest dreams did he think that they would make contact with another intelligent species. He was completely awe-stricken that it was this close to Earth. He thought they would discover simple organisms before their not-so-warm welcome that just threatened them in their own language. How accommodating these aliens were.

"Sounds like we got some buggers down there. Can we exterminate them?" Brad asked.

Everyone turned their head toward Brad in disbelief after he made his reckless statement.

Brad continued, "I know you've run through this scenario before leaving Earth. You must have weapons in place to clear obstructions for our new home."

"Absolutely not!" Isaac said, trying to shut down this stream of thought immediately. "You knew my terms before we even left Earth. We are not to interfere with intelligent life."

"Well, do we at least have some sort of defense system in place? You had to have thought that through if you're not going on the offense. Something to shoot down a projectile from an alien army." Brad said, realizing Isaac probably had more protocols in place to protect himself from his own crew than an outside force like this. How shortsighted.

Isaac's grimace drew perplexing looks from the crew.

Usha's leg bounced nervously at the lack of an answer until she finally said, "I'm sure we can negotiate with them. There must be things we can learn from each other. Countries on Earth have coexisted with each other mostly peacefully for years. Maybe we can settle on another planet in this solar system?"

Isaac looked like he was weighing out all the options for proceeding and reread the last few lines of the cryptic message. Isaac asked, "Karina, when was the message received?"

Karina answered, "The message was received three days ago when we first achieved orbit around the planet."

One by one, the crew turned their attention to the window facing the planet as a fast-moving object appeared to leave the atmosphere heading right toward them. They were a sitting duck. There was no action they could take that would prevent a weapon moving at this speed from a direct impact. Chaos ensued as everyone rose to their feet and paced back and forth, as if heading to the escape pods that didn't exist. There was absolutely nothing they could do as the object got larger and larger as it approached. Just as all hope was lost, the projectile lost thrust and began its slow descent back toward the planet to burn up into the atmosphere.

Another message appeared.

"We gave you three days to respond. This was a warning shot. The next one won't miss. Respond immediately or prepare to meet your end."

They needed to buy time before they could figure out their next course of action.

Isaac replied, "Greetings. Our sincerest apologies. We awoke from our suspended animation three days ago when your message was received and have just now recovered to reply. We intend no harm and are only seeking an additional home to start a new human settlement away from our home planet, Earth. I'm positive that we can come to an agreement. We can provide the knowledge it takes for you to leave your planet's extreme gravity while you can provide a temporary or permanent abode for my crew. Please, no more projectiles until we can peacefully work this out."

The tension in the room had turned to eleven. Everyone continued to pace back and forth as if it would help. The suspense in waiting for their reply was pure agony. Their first message must have been premeditated as they monitored their approach. In contrast, the alien species were most likely taking time to decipher the message and reply appropriately in a human dialect foreign to them.

The message finally appeared.

"Intend no harm? Is it peace and refuge you seek?

We've seen how your species handles peace through your incautious broadcast you've been transmitting into the universe for decades. World wars, nuclear bombs, mass starvation, and poverty that can easily be solved. Instead, they're used as a bargaining chip for politics throughout your existence. You may have left most of your people behind but you are no different from those still on Earth. We have focused all of our attention creating a perfect world here and all you're after is contaminating other worlds with your pestilent mindset. Leave now and never return. Do not inform anyone of our existence."

Negotiating with this intelligent life wasn't going to yield any results. It was a shame they wouldn't be able to learn anything from the alien beings or share what they knew. They probably had all different types of material science, produced by their adaptation to high gravity, that they could learn from. The crew could have potentially helped them in propulsion methods to help leave their planet's surface. So much engineering progress could be made by both sides.

Isaac replied, "There is no need for another projectile. Please give us a few hours to map our next trajectory."

"Karina, plot our course to the next solar system," Isaac announced, sounding utterly defeated. "We don't want them lobbing another explosive at us that actually hits this time."

"Trajectory has been plotted to our next star system. We will begin thrust in seventy-nine minutes when we are in the correct position in orbit."

Brad was back in his quarters, laying on his bed and

staring at the ceiling. He tried to process the events of the day. Being chased away from a super Earth-like planet by an alien being, who thought they were morally superior to the crew, really had Brad thinking about what life would be like on that planet. Looking at the imagery taken while they orbited the planet revealed a surface covered mostly by water, which was much calmer than the oceans humans were used to. Going to the beach on this planet would involve much more sunbathing and much less thrill-seeking, like surfing and boogie boarding that Brad enjoyed.

On the land in this world, activities like running and lifting weights would be a much tougher task. Running a short distance or even walking could feel like completing a marathon for earthling's feeble bodies, which are used to Earth's modest gravity. A human's skeleton would most likely be able to handle the pressure, although their organs would shift and fail while trying to keep their bodies going.

Moving to a world like this would most likely be fatal. However, life that started there seemed to have evolved to adapt to the increased effects of gravity.

All the creatures seemed much shorter than most of the species seen on Earth. The imagery revealed the intelligent beings had an average height of less than one meter and were much stockier than the tall lanky meat bags of their home planet. If only the crew could have challenged these creatures to a basketball game for a winner takes control of the planet competition—in Earth gravity of course. Other creatures on the planet were also shorter and seemed to have a much more protective skin to shield them from outside threats.

The different threats would be greater there. One being the smaller magnetic field protecting the planet from solar winds. More radiation would enter the atmosphere and certainly create a higher risk of cancer for their thin layer of skin. This would increase the need for underground dwellings. There must be more than meets the eye from the overhead imagery. Less of a magnetic field would also mean there might be little or no auroras at the north and south poles. How boring.

There was more of an atmosphere on this planet that would create a more stable climate. This could make citizens in the northeast of the United States long for the changing leaf colors they'd grown so accustomed to. The increased gravity could also create more of a risk for asteroid strikes, much like the increase in the number of strikes on Jupiter in their home star system. The alien's defense system they had developed made perfect sense.

Brad continued to contemplate these aliens during a long hot shower. He settled in his private quarters until footsteps headed down the hall toward him. There was a pause outside of his door, then a slow knock.

"Just a minute," Brad said awkwardly as he rushed to throw on some clothes, knocking over a few things on his desk on the way to the door. "Captain, good thing you knocked or I might have given you a little show. Is there something in your pocket or are you just happy to see me? And what's behind your back?"

Isaac presented the bottle of a Highland Park fifteen-year scotch from behind his back and asked, "Can I come in?"

"Not until you tame that thing down there," Brad said as he pointed down to Isaac's pants and looked off into the distance.

"Oh, those are shot glasses. We need something to drink out of and I didn't have enough hands to hold them."

"That's what they all say. Come on in. I would have tidied the place up a bit more if I knew I was going to have company."

Isaac walked in, sat down at Brad's desk, the only place to sit in their confined quarters, situated the two glasses, and poured the scotch.

"My favorite, you must have really read my files before we left," Brad said adoringly.

"I read everyone's files, and you seemed to be the person who I could really just blow some steam off with," Isaac said. He didn't want to reveal his true intentions before they had some liquid courage.

"I guess I can be good at one thing, at least."

They talked about politics and sports and everything else two individuals who didn't know each other very well could talk about. They slowly let their guard down as the liquid in the bottle disappeared. Brad's brain grew muddled, he worried about making a fool of himself.

"I read your files for more of a reason than to just figure out your favorite drink of choice. What's your story?" Isaac asked. "Why are you really out here? Running from something? Is it the last place where no one can find you?"

"The whole story?" Brad asked and raised his eyebrows. "We're going to need another bottle. I spent my entire life growing up as the perfect child. There was nothing more a parent could want from their offspring. I was a superior athlete and had all the ladies after me. First chair as a flutist in the school orchestra, go ahead, laugh it up. I was a straight-A student all throughout grade school."

"I was always more of a B's and C's get degrees kind of guy myself."

Brad continued, "I maintained this all throughout college, maintaining my status on the Dean's list. I was good enough athletically to get drafted into professional baseball and football if I would so choose to. I even stayed musically inclined, as if all of that wasn't enough. But nothing was good enough for my parents. There was still something missing. I finally snapped and started couch surfing all over the country. Working dead-end jobs and burning bridges wherever I went since I couldn't see the value in pleasing anyone anymore. I could have anything I wanted and decided to have nothing instead. I broke communication with all my friends and relatives and searched for what I wanted."

"Did you ever find what you were looking for?"

"I still haven't until this day. In my late twenties, I realized I wouldn't find what I was looking for out on the road, so I moved back home and tried to mend some relationships with my family. I started running to get my body back into shape, which would hopefully set my mind right as well. It's an activity that almost everyone abhors."

"I sure do hate to run. You're probably the only person on this mission, including our passengers, that enjoy it."

"The hours of isolation with just me, the pavement, and my thoughts put things into perspective. Every time I entered a race, I would spend hours picking people out of the race who I just couldn't let beat me, which propelled me to always get better. I would show up to the finish line completely exhausted, scanning the last hundred meters for a family member or friend who would come out to see me finish, and no one ever came."

"There's more that meets the eye when it comes to you. You never know what people are struggling with internally until you sit down and have a deep conversation with them."

Sometimes a little booze gets that train moving.

Isaac continued, "You may not have found solace in anything or anyone on Earth. All we have is each other up here, and we'll be with you until the end."

"Amen, brother. Good to know. Tales told over what might be the last scotch in the galaxy."

Isaac took a deep breath, slapped his knees, got up forcefully, and said, "Well, I suppose I should be hitting the old dusty trail."

A classic Midwestern goodbye.

Chapter Five

Amy
(Recursive Singularity: Year 425)

"At this point, it's looking like I'm going to be drifting through space until the end of the universe itself."

-The Hypersleep Chronicles

Amy wasn't selected for the main ship of their voyage and that left a sour taste in her mouth. She was still honored to be there on the secondary ship. They were no less important and the main ship didn't have a couple of skill sets they had: her ability to analyze the biology of a new planet and the life-saving abilities of their physician. Mainly, it was the physician.

Amy thought about all the scenarios that could pop up during their travels where they would need to send Raul over on an EVA if disaster struck on the other ship. There could have been a micro meteor strike that went right through the ship and impaled someone. A malfunctioning cryo-sleep chamber that placed someone in a compromised state. A physical injury that resulted from someone going too hard in the gym. Amy needed to stop thinking of all the worst things that could happen. She couldn't help it when thinking of all the plan B scenarios throughout all her years of traveling, especially when traveling solo. Mars was always the plan B for Earth, but it never developed into a fully functioning option that could exist without Earth.

They had arrived at their next stop and it would have been the year 2727 on Earth if it still existed. Seeing another missed message would certainly emphasize the gravity of their situation. Gravity, something they took for granted on Earth. Who knows if they would ever experience planetary gravity again instead of the centrifugal force simulating gravity on the ship. It was time, once again, to check for communications from Earth.

They had all gathered around in the command center, and everyone was afraid to address the elephant in the room.

"Alright, Karina, have we heard from Earth yet?" Victoria reluctantly asked.

The screen lit up and displayed "New SMS message received."

"SMS? We paid for video updates. This will certainly affect our follow-up review," Victoria said with a touch of sarcasm.

"I'll display the message on the screen," Karina said.

"Greetings from Earth. The year is 2710. It's been forty-three years since the bombs rained down. Fermi might have been right; any intelligent species will eventually destroy itself. We hid underground in a bunker we had previously set up in New Zealand. After thirty-six years, we were finally able to return to the surface to rebuild. The climate is different from the perfect habitable Earth you remember.

"Global temperatures dropped by five degrees Celsius as the soot rose into the atmosphere and blocked out the sun. All plant life on the surface was completely obliterated and much of the life in the ocean didn't survive the plunging temperatures. As you can imagine, almost all life on the surface was wiped out. We are still working on regrowing crops with the global seed reserves that made it through the catastrophe.

"Six years ago, we discovered the Tarax data and knew it was necessary to regain communication with every ship that left Earth. We wanted to make sure you keep pressing onward and discourage you from coming back, it's too risky for humans to remain on one planet. We aren't even sure that by the time you receive this message there will be a livable planet to come back to.

"We have been able to send Tarax messages again for the last three months which makes you the second message we are able to send, how lucky for you. It must have been disturbing to not hear from us on your second stop. Unfortunately, we were not able to receive most of the data sent back by these missions. We were hoping to have a whole database full of information from all the planets visited by Tarax missions, unfortunately, this is not the case.

"Our Martian friends are still surviving, barely, and we have been exchanging notes with them on how we can rebuild society. They almost didn't make it as they were still reliant on resupply missions from Earth, however, life always seems to find a way. As a species, we were so terribly close to being completely reliant on Mars as a plan B for the survival of the human race and we had taken that for granted.

"We are rebuilding and should be far along by the time you receive this message. This could have easily been the end of humans if Tarax wouldn't have sent their ships out into space, hopefully some of their ships have found a better world. Keep adventuring, this is proof that life must be spread out among multiple solar systems to remain intact. Don't make the same mistakes we have made on Earth.

"We're hoping to send more spacecrafts out one day as we now see how fragile a single planetary species can be. Keep sending your data so we can learn for future missions and we'll try to stay out of trouble here to actually receive your signals."

The entire reason they were going on this trip was to avoid the fictitious scenario they had just discovered had been the reality on Earth. In hindsight, it would not have happened in Amy's lifetime. Learning that it had happened in billions of other human's lifetimes filled her with a sense of dread she thought unshakable.

Victoria was the first to speak after the dreadful news. "I'm sad to hear about the strife everyone on Earth had to endure. This completely confirms our concerns with humans remaining a single planetary and single solar system species. This is the worst 'I told you so' that we can imagine."

Victoria probably secretly enjoyed having her idea for leaving Earth validated.

Amy wanted to change the subject. "Karina, how are we looking on the planets in this system?"

The screen in the command center displayed the data:

Bolden-121A
Distance (Light Years from Earth): 17.1
Apparent Magnitude: 4.65
Stellar Classification: G6V

Bolden-121B
Distance (Light Years from Earth): 17.1
Apparent Magnitude: 11.38
Stellar Classification: M4V

Bolden-121c
Mass: 0.74
Radius: 0.78
Period (Days): 288

Bolden-121d
Mass: 0.88
Radius: 1.02
Period (Days): 346

Bolden-121e

Mass: 1.28
Radius: 1.48
Period (Days): 412

"Our current solar system is a dual star system, like Kepler-47, or originally made much more popular by the sunset visible on the fictional planet of Tatooine in *Star Wars*. Visible on the main control panel are the star's attributes as well as the three potentially habitable planets orbiting these stars." Victoria said, then paused. "There are two smaller planets closer to our current two host stars spiraling inward toward these two stars, given the mass of the stars collectively. These two planets will most likely not exist in the not-so-distant future. They will be vaporized and vanish below the surface of the star, and it would mostly be unnoticed."

"Maybe like us eventually," Raul mumbled under his breath.

"As we entered the solar system, there were two gas giants located after our potentially habitable worlds," Victoria continued. "Most interestingly, a planet with rings forty-eight times the diameter of the rings on a planet you may remember named Saturn."

"Could you imagine our kids being able to see a planet like that through their backyard telescope?" asked Amy.

"We'll fantasize about that after we get to work and determine if these three Goldilocks planets have potential for us," Victoria replied.

"Goldilocks planets?" asked James.

"You know. Not too hot, not too cold," Amy answered. "Planets right in the proverbial habitable Goldilocks zone. Speaking of Goldilocks zones, it looks like we're picking up some movement in some of our imagery of the closest potentially habitable planet. I'll need to study these images more."

Amy spent half of the day flipping through images of the planet, sipping on coffee, and softly saying things like "amazing" and "magnificent." Most of the crew looked over her shoulder while she worked and paid close attention whenever they heard any of her words of excitement. The crew meandered around the ship as Amy diligently worked for hours until she finally turned around and faced the crew and said, "As a biologist, this is the happiest day of my life. As someone who is trying to find a new home for humans, I am completely devastated."

"Are we going to head over and make some friends?" inquired Raul.

"Not on this planet. There is a wild diversity of plants and animals on this planet, although none of them would rise to the level of using language or using tools. The planet's gravity is much less than that of Earth's so the plant life has soared toward the sky unlike anything we're used to. This also affects the animal life as they have grown much ganglier than the paunchier animals that we're used to like hippos and rhinos. Think of how much taller a giraffe would be on planet Earth if they needed to reach fruit on the much taller trees of this planet. Their eyes are much smaller than the animals we're used to due to the proximity to its star. It's absolutely magnificent."

"I think I could make friends with them," said James.

"I bet you could. I would say you're probably on the same intelligence with them. That wouldn't be very nice to say about them, though. That's neither here nor there. We're all in agreement that we cannot interfere with the natural progress of life and they are undoubtedly on their way to intelligence no matter how you ultimately define it."

"Look at how the USA became such a great nation. They did some terrible things when they initially sailed over, but we wouldn't be here today if it weren't for those awful deeds. This system has a couple of planets that are basically ready for us to conquer and live on," Raul protested.

Victoria replied, "The mishappenings of the past are not to be used as excuses for foul behavior in the future. We've learned an extraordinary amount about life which popped up so close to our original solar system and we will be grateful for that on our way to our next stop in our adventure. There will be no further discussions, class dismissed."

Everyone else, besides Amy and Victoria, headed back to their quarters to get some sleep for the night before they plotted their course the following day. Amy and Victoria were the night owls of the group.

Victoria dropped what she was doing to face Amy and said, "As the biologist of the group, are you disappointed you couldn't go down there and study life on this planet more?"

"I knew I wouldn't have the most hands-on role in the

group while we're up here floating around in space. I'm sure my time will come."

"Your time will come once we finally reach our destination."

"That's what I keep telling myself. I heard Isaac cornered Brad with some whiskey at the first stop. Is there any left? Maybe that'll help me pass the time."

"News really travels fast between two ships where there are only ten people awake. Should I go grab some that Isaac provided for our ship?"

"I'm just joking with you. I'm a recovering alcoholic."

Victoria's brows furrowed, scanning her memories of everyone's files. How could she have missed this? She and Isaac had brought booze on a confined ship where someone had an abusive relationship with alcohol.

"I'm so sorry he brought this temptation along with us," Victoria said in an apologetic tone.

"It's all good. I just like to see people's reactions when I bring that up. When you tell people you don't drink, they look at you like something is wrong with you. It's like telling someone you're not a dog person. They assume you're some sort of psychopath."

"I'm not much of a dog person, so I guess we're both considered a threat to society."

"You heathen! I'm the same way. I'm hoping we didn't bring any with us. I'm tired of pretending I care about people's dogs. It's the only thing people with dogs talk about."

"That's pretty weird with you being a biologist, but I totally get that. When someone shows me a picture of their dog, I just count to five and let out a little phrase of endearment."

"Same. Cats are okay, I guess. I mostly like the bigger ones, though."

"Yeah, they aren't bad. Anyway, if you don't mind me asking, was there a certain event that led to your decision to stop drinking?"

"Not really one occasion, multiple occasions over years of an abusive relationship. I guess it started in college. I came from a small town and didn't really know what the stuff was. I was opened to a whole new world of possibilities when I got to college. I graduated with my bachelor's degree and almost finished a master's program when I started really hitting the bottle. I was afraid to leave my party world behind and getting a master's degree symbolized me needing to be an actual adult in the real world."

"People can really take things too far when they leave the area where they are from and discover a whole new world of possibilities."

"The problem was I stayed near the city where I grew up and it was just like in college with everyone around me, reinforcing my poor behavior. I became a bartender because the tips from my friends were fantastic. I would pull the classic 'only charging them for half of their drinks while they tip me off of what the bill should be' routine. I moved bar to bar as the owners would always eventually catch on to what I was doing. Drinking on my shifts, visiting my other bartender friends when I wasn't working and drinking with them, I was drinking on days that ended with Y, you know?"

"I think I'm picking up what you're putting down."

"I probably spent more time drunk than I was sober. Hooking up with random strangers and friends, passing out in alleyways after beer festivals, not remembering what I had done the second half of the day before. It wasn't a healthy lifestyle at all. I had another bartender friend who was in her mid-forties who looked like she was in her mid-sixties, and I decided once and for all that I couldn't keep going down this dark path. Things really peaked when I passed out one day as I was nursing a hang-over and almost drowned, falling into the harbor near where I worked. I wouldn't be here today if a random per-son jogging by me that day wouldn't have jumped in and saved me."

Victoria raised her hand. "I, for one, am thankful for the jogger."

"Make that two of us. After that event, I walked into work the next day, told them I quit, and I haven't worked in the bar industry since. I read books to pass the time in-stead of spending all of my money out on the town. Those first science fiction novels I read saved my life. The next semester I went back to college to finish the master's de-gree I started, which led me on this path to you. I still drink every once in a while, on special occasions. How-ever, I always keep myself to a three-beverage rule. Quit-ting things absolutely works for some people. I believe that moderation in all things is the best policy."

"Thank you so much for sharing that with me. I might take you up on that three-drink policy once we reach our final destination."

"I'll hold you to it. How about you, what's your story?"

"I guess you could say, like how you were a big fan of alcohol, I was quite the workaholic on Earth."

"It seems like there's a correlation with that and being space commanders."

"I wasn't quite on Isaac's level. It all started with my first hourly job at the local utility company. I was being paid by the hour and would do anything for that sweet time and a half and double time on the weekends. I would do anything in my power to work late in the office or be on call to work storm duty shifts during the nights and weekends. As I worked my way up at different companies, I couldn't get rid of that mentality even when I was being paid a salary wage. I knew I wasn't being paid anymore by working additional hours, but I couldn't stop working to get ahead and make a bigger wage."

Amy wanted to lighten the mood and said, "Not quite like the results of drinking too much alcohol, although I can see how that's also problematic."

"I shouldn't really be complaining. It was quite detrimental to my social life, though. I saw every person as someone I could use to get ahead and treated everyone in my life like they were a pawn in my game. It was all so liberating when I finally received the call to be a part of this mission. I worked every moment of every day until that call came through and then I just stopped everything I was doing to make this dream a reality. A switch in my brain really flipped that day."

"As long as you left that lifestyle behind. I mean, it's very great to have someone like that around, given the weight of the scenario we're in now. It might be problematic if you keep that going on in our eventual new world."

"There are still aspects of that in my life, although I like to think I'm completely in remission."

"That makes two of us. I think I'm going to head back to my quarters. All this people-ing really takes it out of me sometimes. I'd rather just be with animals, the wild ones, that is."

Chapter Six

Usha
(Arbitrary Algorithm: Year 490)

"Maybe this is my purgatory, waiting in a plane on a runway that may never take off to deliver me toward my final judgment."

-The Hypersleep Chronicles

The wake-up process seemed brand new every single time until that third day when it all started coming back. It made Usha think about the many therapy sessions she had to complete each week back on Earth, usually about twenty-five hours of them, and how she didn't know what she was walking into every single time.

Usha was mostly involved in family therapy, so it was more about telling the parents what they were doing wrong instead of addressing the concerns about their children. She would have sessions that went well and improve with each consecutive meeting, until a family threw her a curveball out of nowhere. Parents bragged about the progress their kids were making in one session, then scream at her the next for the smallest inconvenience like a scheduling error. The fast-paced schedule was not for her. She should have stuck with screening patients instead of doing therapy sessions.

It would have been the year 2792 on Earth and Usha, along with the entire crew, was really missing that place.

Usha wasn't sure if she was getting used to the process, but something seemed different at this location. It was the same food they had been struggling to get down. However, it was fresher today. The coffee was more robust and gave her a whole new pep in her step. It was like that fourth or fifth consecutive therapy session she'd have with a family before that inevitable curveball sailed across home plate. She eagerly went over to the window to see if she could wave at one of her crew members on the other ship.

Staring out into the vastness of space could be a terrifying or promising experience, depending on how it was schematized. When looking out into any direction, there were hundreds of thousands of bright dots. Each represented a host star that could have hosted millions of years of evolution. Each speck of light represented the opportunity for life that could have become intelligent, just as their species had on Earth. Every small point is perhaps a location where civilizations have come and gone without making their presence known on the interstellar stage, as far as she knew. It gives a person the conviction that this was the right path in life, to ensure the permanence of a species that can fully understand its existence in the universe.

A numbing terror crept over her. Usha was taken back to an experience in her childhood when she was playing fetch with her beloved Jack Russell terrier, Jackson, on a foggy morning. She had launched the ball out into the mist as she had many times before, but this time, the sound of her pet's collar stopped making noise. Her pet never returned from the fog after that toss.

Instead of moving her eyes slowly from star to star, collecting light from each star that most likely took millions of years to reach her, she frantically looked around the empty void in front of her. Something was wrong here.

"Karina, open communications with the other ship," Usha said as she tried to hide her concern.

The crew couldn't avoid hearing the struggle in her voice as she asked the question.

After a long pause, Isaac inquired again, "Karina, where is the other ship?"

"There is no sign of the other ship within this solar system," Karina answered.

"What …" Justine struggled to ask the question and finally continued, "What could have possibly happened to them?"

"Space travel is dangerous. There are several things that could have happened," Isaac replied as he counted on his fingers as if listing all the different scenarios in his head.

"I didn't sign up for this, none of us did," Usha muttered under her breath as she seemed to plead with a higher power.

"We all signed up for this, and we knew there was always the possibility we wouldn't even make it to our first stop," Isaac said.

"It's a little different experiencing it firsthand," said Justine.

"This doesn't mean they're dead, right? They could have just experienced a technical difficulty with the ship and had to lag behind in order to fix it, right?" asked Usha.

"That's possible. There are a lot of things that can go wrong with interstellar travel. They have Stephanie on the ship who should be able to handle any situation," Brad said.

"Should we wait for them?" asked Usha.

"We don't have any record of what went wrong. There must have been some sort of glitch in the ship's software and they don't have their own computer scientist on their ship," Justine said.

"There isn't really much we can do here but continue with the mission," Isaac interrupted. "Karina, show us what we have here."

"Once again we have no signal from Earth," replied Karina.

The screen in the command center displayed the data:

Lovell-286
Distance (Light Years from Earth): 19.4
Apparent Magnitude: 8.16
Stellar Classification: M1V

Lovell-286c
Mass: 0.68
Radius: 0.92
Period (Days): 6

Lovell-286d
Mass: 1.03
Radius: 1.22
Period (Days): 9

Lovell-286e
Mass: 1.35
Radius: 1.41
Period (Days): 13

"Tinah, we could really go for some good news. What kind of good news do we have?" Isaac asked.

"This star, Lovell-286, is a red dwarf star. I would like to say that the grass is greener on this side, however, the vegetation here would look different on these planets. Photosynthesis would be altered on this planet from what we're used to on Earth to adjust to the different wavelengths of photons coming from this red dwarf star."

"I bet the leaves changing in the fall would be extraordinary," Justine said, staring off into the distance. "I guess this wouldn't help folks who are red-green colorblind, though."

"Our retinas would most likely need to evolve differently to deal with these different photons, so unfortunately, no help for those folks. They already miss out on the deep reds and oranges of the sunsets back on Earth. There would be even more lack of appreciation for the much deeper hues of red with a sunset on these hunks of rocks," Tinah explained.

"These terms seem acceptable, just a little color shift. I'm assuming there's a catch to this system, though?" Usha asked. She thought they would have found a place to live by now and was hoping there wasn't a catch.

"The first planet is pretty close to this star and is tidally locked to it, kind of like how Luna is tidally locked to the Earth," Tinah continued. "One side of the planet is constantly being berated by light and radiation from Lovell-286 which has turned it into a dry desert wasteland. There's very little chance that much besides an extremophile elite can live under these conditions."

"Do you think we would find some sandworms if we went down on that side of the planet?" asked Brad.

Tinah shot Brad a puzzled look and replied, "You never know. I would say no. The other side of the planet is permanently plunged into darkness. Your parents wouldn't be able to tell you to come home when the streetlights turn on because they would just always be on. There's little chance that anything could survive on this side either, though, maybe even less of a chance than on the sunny side of the planet."

"Probably less of a chance of sexually transmitted infections than the nightlife you're used to," Justine said and nudged Brad's arm with her elbow.

Brad glanced at Isaac as if he would defend him. Isaac couldn't hold back a laugh and said, "That's kind of funny."

Tinah stood up to gain the attention of everyone and said, "Life could survive on the small strip of land in between these two extremes where an eternal twilight exists. Ice on the dark side would be slowly and continuously melting and streaming into the hot side through ravines which could sustain some sort of life. Not exactly where I would want to live. At least there's no argument to bring back daylight savings time. Just as our luck has been going, this is the only planet that we might survive on right away. The other two planets would take a bit of work terraforming before we could even consider moving to a life we are used to back on Earth with sunrises and seasons."

"I don't like where this conversation is heading," Brad said.

"The second planet is experiencing a runaway greenhouse effect, much like Venus was in our old neighborhood. The planet here is still in the earlier stages of this effect and it would take a bit of effort to remove all the carbon dioxide from the air and to reduce the three-hundred-degree Celsius temperatures. The third planet is the opposite, much like good old Mars that we know and love. We would need to do the reverse of that to create an atmosphere and warm up the planet. This is still an ongoing argument back home on whether we can set off some kind of nuclear reaction at the poles or set up a giant mirror to deflect the sun to melt the ice caps to achieve this goal.

Either way, it would take an effort to do, which I'm assuming they have still not done on Mars to this day."

"This is not the way I want to live out the rest of my life and would not give me a warm and fuzzy feeling about the continuity of the human race even if we made progress here in my lifespan," Isaac said as he looked around the room and everyone agreed with him. There wasn't complete confidence in everyone's reactions as they avoided eye contact with each other.

"Can we bookmark it for later?" asked Usha.

"If it would make you feel better, we will put it in the proverbial parking lot for later," Isaac replied.

Usha headed to Isaac's room near the end of the day after he had requested her. Tensions had been on the rise with the crew on the ship, and everyone was acting a little strange. She felt like she was heading to the principal's office for interrogation after some of her friends were accused of misbehaving in class.

Usha opened his slightly cracked door, "Hey commander, you wanted to see me?"

"Yes, please come in. Have a seat." Isaac was sitting on his bed, bouncing his leg as she sat down, avoiding eye contact.

"You seem different than usual. Is there something bothering you? Have you ever seen a therapist before?"

"I wouldn't say bothering, just something I was hoping to get to the bottom of. Am I supposed to lie down like they do in movies and whatnot? I've never done this before."

"Whatever is comfortable with you, don't feel you have to conform to societal norms."

"I'm going to lie down, not because it's what everyone else does, just because I want to. I've been having these dreams that have been evolving since we've left Proxima Centauri."

"How often do you experience this problem?"

"They usually happen on the third night when we arrive at any new location and I'm not sure what they mean or if it's some type of prophecy. I certainly don't want these scenarios to become a self-fulfilling prophecy, or start doubting myself because of what I've seen."

"Sure, you're not the first to come to me with concerns about their dreams."

"Alright, I was walking up to the window and glancing out at the Recursive Singularity. One of my favorite sights is seeing it drift so effortlessly through space, carrying our fellow crew members. It seems like it was one of their favorite things also since I see them all standing at their window, staring back at me and waving. I didn't think I would be able to see them this well since we keep quite a distance away while traveling at these immense speeds. Knowing there are others out here with us on this journey brings a certain comfort that's hard to describe. An object approached their spacecraft in the distance and it grew larger and larger by the second. I pointed at it and I shouted through the communications system to warn them of their impending doom, but they didn't notice my frantic warnings. They just continued to wave and smile and feed off my chaotic energy as if they couldn't hear my trepidation."

"How did that make you feel about yourself?" Usha inquired; she rubbed her chin as if she was taming a beard that she didn't have.

"I felt ignored and completely unheard. Like I was trying to do everything I could for my crew and it wasn't working. The silent assassin careening toward them just kept getting larger and larger until it made contact with their vessel. The rotating section of their craft erupted where the asteroid made contact, sucking everything in the immediate area into the vacuum of space. The crew continued to make eye contact with me in despair, wondering why I wouldn't warn them about their terrible fate. One by one, they lost their grips, launched toward the opening created by the asteroid. The opening was directed toward the Arbitrary Algorithm and they slowly got ejected from their ship, drifting across the empty void in between us."

"Does this cause any insomnia?"

"The terror in some of these situations does tend to keep me up sometimes. They eventually accumulated on the outside of the window where I was so desperately trying to warn them about the projectile heading toward them. I could do nothing for them in the short few minutes that they would be able to survive before they succumbed to the cruel fate of the vacuum of space. They pleaded with me to let them on board and they cursed me for leading them on this suicide mission."

Usha crossed her legs and nodded in reassurance for

him to continue.

"Stephanie pleaded with me first in the dream, 'I left my husband behind because I believed in your mission. How could you lead me on a suicide mission?' Raul followed, 'I promised my parents that I was sacrificing my life on Earth for the greater good of humanity. It was all for nothing.' Finally, 'It's all your fault!' Victoria was screaming at me."

"How does the dream end?"

"Then I finally figured it out. How am I hearing them when there isn't any medium in space for sound to travel through? I'm having dreams like these on the third day at every new location. I had this dream right before the events that took place today. What's wrong with me, doc?" Isaac pleaded with her as he raised both of his hands to his head and rubbed his scalp.

"It's perfectly understandable to have doubts," Usha said and placed her hand on his shin and gave it a squeeze of reassurance. "Dreams are our way of sorting out all the information and emotions that we experience throughout the day."

"I've always been a lucid dreamer. I feel like telling you this is like looking out of the window in a plane, pointing out to the passenger next to you that there are millions of tiny parts that had to do their job just right to keep you alive."

"While they may seem quite disturbing, it is not at all unheard of that people coming out of a long hibernation can have extreme nightmares due to your body trying to catch up on restful sleep."

"It feels better already just to get that off of my chest. Do you promise to not tell anyone else? I can't have anyone thinking that I am having second thoughts. I need to be fearless in front of my crew."

"Of course, client confidentiality applies to the universe, not just Earth."

"That's great to hear. How about you? Any secrets you've been dying to not be the only person with knowledge of? Life stories? Deepest regrets? You have always been very stoic; I want to know the real you."

"Not many people besides you know this about me, but I cannot have children. My usefulness to the crew outweighed this in the selection process."

Usha had a moment to reflect on this, as Isaac reprocessed this fact. Everyone riding along was carefully selected because they were all fertile and featured the perfect combination of dominant and recessive traits that were split evenly among the two ships. The original plan for two ships carrying 255 passengers was based on the minimum viable population 50/500 rule. The minimum population required to prevent inbreeding would be fifty and the minimum population to prevent genetic drift was five hundred. The five-hundred rule was based on genetic drift caused by random chance that would cause gene variations to disappear and eventually reduce overall genetic variation.

There were 255 people now with the loss of the Recursive Singularity, which, although it was enough for a sustainable breeding structure, it would be a lot of coordination. Therefore, they wouldn't be able to leave this process up to random chance.

Unfortunately, everyone on their new planet would not be able to afford the luxury of procreating with exactly who they wanted if they were to be successful for many generations to come. Everyone could marry whoever they wanted at this point, however, baby making would need to have a procedure that was strictly adhered to. Once their numbers increased over the generations, they would eventually be able to leave things up to chance.

Usha continued, "All my life, I grew up playing with dolls and wanting a little child of my own to take care of and raise. I come from a large family and seeing my happy grandparents with everyone around them to take care of them, I wanted an even bigger family when I was old. I've been through many relationships and have had to endure everyone asking me when I would have children. I had finally met the perfect person, and we tried to have kids. However, the body I was given just wasn't going to cooperate with me; what a bad hand I was dealt with from the beginning and didn't even know it. My husband left me and so began my journey here. I wanted to devote my life to creating opportunities in new worlds for others to expand into giant families like I had always wanted."

"I'm so sorry to hear that. Even if you don't have your own kids to take care of you, the crew and I will always be around to support you and never leave your side."

"That's the second-best thing I could ever hope for."

"Thanks for listening to my concerns and giving me reassurance to continue into the unknown."

Chapter Seven

The Regulator
(Arbitrary Algorithm: Year 571)

"As commander of the Arbitrary Algorithm, I made the decision I had to in order to ensure the success of the mission."

-The Hypersleep Chronicles

Isaac was surprised at how quickly the experience they all shared at the last stop had shifted the mood of the entire crew. Tinah was an astute educator, but she wasn't too enthusiastic about their last stop to offer her usual fun facts and planet scenarios. Usha had graced him with the unexpected therapy session, though she was no longer providing her off-the-cuff words of encouragement, helping to keep everyone optimistic and focused on the mission. Brad wasn't the most optimistic as it was, but he no longer provided the crew with his underappreciated dark humor that made things more light-hearted when they needed to be. Similarly, Justine wasn't getting in her usual jabs at the expense of Brad that had everyone besides Karina cracking up.

There was an ominous vibe throughout the ship that no one could even attempt to avoid. Isaac needed a victory soon or the crew would start losing faith in his mission. Isaac contemplated all the different team-building activities he had forced his employees to participate in over the years. His ace, the classic pizza party, would not be an option out here in the great unknown. Good luck on a delivery driver finding them here, he thought.

The food got old at their fourth stop on this journey. Isaac hoped they would find somewhere to stay by now, although it was a possibility they would never find somewhere too. There were five options for food ready at the press of a button and a three-minute wait: Jollof rice, chicken tikka masala, jambalaya, flautas, and chicken tenders. The chicken fingers were so big that they were more like chicken hands. Though all the options were unique, they all tasted the same.

This food was made to keep them alive and offer no enjoyment in the process. Isaac wished he would have brought some Old Bay with him. That is one spice that has stood the test of time.

Isaac daydreamed about the world they would eventually explore and that it would compare to the Earth in the late Devonian era, the Age of the Fish. Isaac just hoped to not experience what Earth had seen at the end of that era. There was a great diversity of shrubs and trees that littered the landscape. There were no animals roaming the land, but most likely, a sprouting diversity of life lived underneath the ocean's surface. It would be Isaac's job now, since Amy wasn't there, to find out just how far along this diversification extended.

Many fish were most likely in the sea, which would be perfect to add to a nutritional diet that they all desperately needed. Regardless, it was important to proceed with caution on the fish front. There must be studies done to make sure of the short-term and long-term effects of consuming this alien source of calories. Also, it would be reckless to throw off the balance of life in the oceans by their presence. The safest way to proceed was to create a fish farm using the preselected fish brought with them from Earth.

Isaac imagined a conversation going on at their eventual new home. Tinah was yelling down the hall of the ship to Brad, "Can you grab the fish and bring them outside? We're ready for them."

"Oh, I already took care of them and gave them a proper funeral in the latrine earlier today." Brad replied as he walked up with the fish.

"Very funny, that reminds me of when we were kids. We had our neighbor watch our fish for us while we were away on vacation. Long story short, our neighbor forgot about the fish and my parents provided them with a proper burial when we got home. I'll never forget you, Goldie."

"Goldie, classic name. I can just see these fish when they boarded our spacecraft before we left. It probably looked like that scene from *Noah's Ark,* where they walked hand in hand up the ramp holding hands in sets of twos."

"I really hope you're joking. They're fish, they can swim, they don't need to be on the ark."

"Right, I was just testing you," Brad said and quickly changed the subject.

Salmon and Atlantic mackerel were the two fish choices that would be the first sustainable animal food source. These were some of the most nutritional fish back on Earth and were quickly reproducing species that would be able to support a growing population until they could get a feel for the interconnected biosphere of this planet. They placed the fish in two separate large tanks set up near their meat cultivating lab. One tank had water that they brought along with them, and the other contained the water from the river that ran through their new town.

Isaac snapped back from his daydream, looking out of the spacecraft's window, which gave everyone in the crew such a grim feeling now. He could sense the emptiness and loneliness in everyone since they were now the only ship on this mission, and possibly the only ship still in existence that had left Earth. Even taking into account their fellow ship was gone and realizing this every time he looked out, something else was wrong when Isaac looked out into the vast emptiness of space.

Isaac sat unmoving in the command center, oblivious his crew had slipped in one at a time until the last person entered.

"It is the year 2873 on Earth right now. What's going on with that place?" Isaac asked.

"Once again we have no signal from Earth," replied

Karina.

The crew groaned and gazed around each other, their faces grim, contemplating the unspoken concern that weighed heavily in the air.

"That's happened before. It's concerning. We must press onward with the mission, though," Isaac declared. Isaac wanted to share with everyone the dread he was feeling and the terrifying dreams he had been experiencing. Regardless, he had to show strength in these defining moments.

"I'm wishing I would have just lived out my mediocre life on Earth at this point," Brad said with a gloomy demeanor, "we know Earth was going to last at least that long now after receiving our first message at Proxima Centauri."

"We're here now. Complaining about the past isn't going to make anything better. Karina, give us the update on our current location," Isaac said and looked toward the big monitor.

Karina replied, "Here is a read-out of our current star and potential homes."

The screen in the command center displayed the data:

Bolden-187
Distance (Light Years from Earth): 22.1
Apparent Magnitude: 2.63
Stellar Classification: G2V

Bolden-187c

Mass:
Radius:
Period (Days):

Bolden-187d
Mass:
Radius:
Period (Days):

Bolden-187e
Mass: 1.46
Radius: 2.1
Period (Days): 602

"I'm no expert, but I'm thinking that can't be good," said Brad.

"Now that you mention it; I thought it was a little strange that I didn't see anything outside of the windows when we woke up, you know, like the usual planet we wake up to," said Isaac.

Red lights and loud alarms filled the room.

"Warning. Approaching asteroid field. Warning. Approaching asteroid field."

Isaac had a brief thought that it was weird to hear a robot voice that wasn't Karina's.

"There's our answer. It seems like our first two habitable planets may have gotten a little too close to each other and had a collision creating some debris," Isaac said.

"We have an asteroid belt back home. Why isn't it nice and peaceful like that one?" asked Usha. Her voice rose higher and higher in pitch as her question trailed on as if trying to appease the asteroids.

"Jupiter's gravity keeps most of the asteroids back home from entering the inner solar system and keeps Earth safe for the most part. There must not be anything like that here," replied Justine.

"Warning. Approaching asteroid field. Warning. Approaching asteroid field."

"That's just fan-freakin-tastic," Brad said as he threw his hands in the air. "Do we really have time for this science lesson? What do we do now?"

Isaac's frustration was at an all-time high. He was trying not to let it show. Isaac said, "Karina, why didn't you bring this up earlier?"

"You weren't in the correct mental state to make decisions concerning the safety of the crew and it wasn't an emergency yet," Karina stated. "Now, you're in the correct mental state."

There was a brief pause.

"It's also now an emergency," replied Karina in her monotonal, unconcerned voice.

"Warning. Approaching asteroid field. Warning. Approaching asteroid field."

"Thanks! I realize that! Will the spacecraft's shields hold? I know what happened to the other ship," Isaac said.

Karina replied, "There are two options. First, we continue on our current path through the asteroid field, chance of survival is set at four percent."

"That sounds like a terrible option. What's option two?" Isaac frantically asked.

"Second, we change our course to avoid the planetary debris, chance of survival is set at eighty-six percent."

"Warning. Approaching asteroid field. Warning. Approaching asteroid field."

"There must be a catch. What's the catch?"

"We will be far off our predetermined path set forth with Tarax and will most likely lose contact with the Earth for the foreseeable future. We use gravity assists from the planets to slingshot us onto the next destination, and we will lose our momentum and be far off of our course. Anyone on this ship will most certainly never hear from Earth again."

Isaac had left little behind on Earth in the way of meaningful relationships and wasn't worried about cutting ties with whoever was left there. He didn't take any time at all to think about how others in the crew might feel about most likely never hearing from Earth ever again.

"Warning. Approaching asteroid field. Warning. Approaching asteroid field."

"Option two, now!" Isaac commanded.

Seconds dragged on in excruciating silence until Karina replied, "Course corrected."

Isaac felt like he was now at the Pacific Ocean's Point Nemo, the very heart of the South Pacific Gyre. The oceanic pole of inaccessibility that covers thirty-seven million square kilometers of ocean on Earth. Their vessel was floating thousands of kilometers from any other person or land mass without an anchor. A spacecraft floating through complete nothingness that had once been tethered to their home base, Earth. Isaac's eyes dimmed, feeling as insignificant in this moment as a shooting star when he had initially learned they were, in fact, not stars, just regular little hunks of rocks burning up in Earth's atmosphere.

"I feel like we should have discussed this a little more as a group," interjected Brad.

"I agree with eighty-six percent over four percent. A discussion between everyone would have been preferred," added Tinah.

"I'm the commander, which means I have the final word over decisions regarding the safety and future of this mission. Everyone agreed to this before we left!" Isaac exclaimed.

"And look at where that has gotten us! No new home yet and now we're left without a hope for any future communication with our home base. We should have stayed on the Bolden-121 star system and conquered that unintelligent life when we had the chance. I say we head straight back there and take what could easily be ours," contested Brad.

Riled up by that statement, Justine replied, "There is no way that I can allow you to do that. Christopher Columbus already got canceled in the early 2000s for what he did and I will not be a part of a crew that would participate in similar behavior and receive a similar reputation."

"We should have just stayed at Lovell-286 where we at least had a fighting chance," Usha interrupted. "We know we would have survived on at least one planet while not stepping on the toes of aliens and could have made steady progress toward spreading out onto the other planets."

"Let's take a vote and decide as a group," said Brad.

"There will be no votes. Everyone signed up for this. Remember the contracts you signed with me?" Isaac said rhetorically.

"And who is left in existence to enforce those contracts? Everyone raise your hands if you think we should all contribute to making decisions from here on out?" Brad asked while looking around the room, hand raised.

There was a reluctance from everyone to participate as their commander stared at them each individually for a length of time. First, Tinah raised her hand, avoiding eye contact with Isaac. Next, Justine pointed a finger up toward the ceiling, showing her desire to have shared power. Everyone was now staring at Usha, who had been trying to maintain the faith in the current system of authority which had held the group together.

"They're not wrong. Let's get together on all decisions and take a vote before moving forward. We did sign contracts, as you mentioned. Who is going to enforce that contract? The Earth? The other ship? Both of which we've lost contact with on this death odyssey," replied Usha.

"Alright. I can't control how you all feel. We'll start governing as a group here. Starting at our next solar system, we can all have an equal say on whether each stop will become our new home. You'll all eventually see how this is a flawed system and can put us in danger in a situation like we just went through," Isaac stated.

Everyone breathed an air of relief, feeling their fates

belong in their own collective hands once again. The tension in Brad's body finally eased after having started the rebellion, not sure if everyone else would go along with his stunt. One by one, each member slowly ventured back to their sleep tanks to prepare for the next solar system where they would have more of a say about their future.

Isaac felt so terribly betrayed.

His crew had collapsed in on him like how a massive dying star's nuclear fusion loses the fight with its immense gravitational forces to create a black hole. There was now a black hole in his chest where his heart used to be. Nothing besides Hawking radiation could escape the grip of a black hole. The crew would not be able to overcome what Isaac had in store for them. Isaac confidently strolled back to his cryo-sleep chamber, knowing for certain that he would not let anyone have shared authority over the decision that would impact the future of his ship. Isaac didn't work his entire life, struggling all the way from the bottom, just to see his empire topple down around him because his crew didn't agree with his vision.

From the beginning, Isaac would find their new home or die trying. The features that Tarax installed on the ship for Isaac before he left would make sure that the mission would be completed one way or another.

Chapter Eight

The Hypersleep Chronicles

Commander's Log (Earth Year 2981): It was a common feature for a Tarax spacecraft to have the option for its commander to keep everyone else in suspended animation and for only the commander to wake up at the next stop. There were many reasons for this: rationing supplies, potential mutiny, etc. This was a well-kept secret between each mission's commander and the Tarax Corporation. If everyone knew about this feature, no one would ever sign up to venture out into the galaxy, so it had to remain confidential. As commander of the Arbitrary Algorithm, I made the decision I had to in order to ensure the success of the mission. If I'm successful, I'm sure the crew will understand and accept the decision I have made. If I'm not successful, they may never find out about what I've done. That is not an option.

At the end of the day, democracy is really just a mob mentality. The mob that was my crew was hysterical and could not be trusted to make choices when such a decision like the future of the mission was to be decided. There was most likely not an Earth still around to go back to, so it would be an unnecessary risk to head back there to see what was going on, and it seemed like that's what the crew wanted to do. Every stop on this trip will need to be made with a purpose, and the purpose will be to discover a new home, not the one we left.

I am slightly worried about my mental state while being alone on the ship without human interaction to keep me sane. I'm not sure if you can see these messages, Karina, so I just want to make it clear I appreciate your company. Regardless, it can't replace relationships with actual humans. I'm not sure how long this mission will drag out, so I'll continue to keep these journal entries to keep my thoughts documented and hopefully to ward off insanity. Maybe these entries will be found one day and they'll make a book out of them. They can call them *The Deep-Sleep Diaries.* No, *The Hypersleep Chronicles*.

The first stop by myself has turned out to be like our fourth stop, which is much better than I can say about some of the other situations. This is not a star I would want to settle down in, but at least there were no tragedies and we're all alive to continue pressing on. Time to put myself back into hibernation. I guess I'm going to miss the turning of the new millennium on Earth while I'm in hibernation en route to my next stop. If there are any humans left on Earth, I wonder if there will be the same Y3K scares like there were for Y2K. Happy new millennium, Earth!

Commander's Log (Earth Year 3348): It's been a few stops since my first entry. I thought it was silly that I was keeping a little diary like I'm some kind of middle school kid. It will be important to look back on these depending on the overall outcome of the mission. Each destination has been just as boring as the one before it. There's been a couple of stars with potential planets and livable moons. They just weren't meeting my initial guidelines.

I know the perfect star system is out there. I'm going to find it or die trying. I feel slightly guilty that I'm dragging these seemingly lifeless souls along with me, but they will thank me for my efforts in the end. No one else would have the willpower and determination to do what I'm doing and it will pay off in the end. Or it won't. At least no one will be around to say I told you so, right?

Commander's Log (Earth Year 3771): I haven't been exercising like I used to since I decided to deep freeze and abandon my crew members. I might as well make good use of the couple of days that I am awake and fully aware at each stop. I feel like this is affecting my mental health, so I am writing down my new routine to encourage myself to stick to it.

If the star system I visit violates my first rule, it's a rowing and running stop. Running hasn't always been my favorite activity and rowing should provide more of a full-body workout to activate all of my muscles. If the star system violates my second rule, it's a strength training stop. We'll do a push-pull workout and get everything activated. Deadlifts, bench press, squats, and overhead press. If it violates my third requirement, it's burpees. Does my hatred for burpees correlate with the fact that none of the stars I've mapped out should violate my third rule? Probably.

This stop turned out to be a cardio stop. It's always so hard to get started, although once you get going you might as well keep going. I would alternate back and forth between running and rowing to keep my muscles guessing. Ten minutes of running, five minutes of rowing, ten minutes of running, five minutes of rowing, and ten minutes of running. Rowing is the ultimate team sport; everyone needs to be both physically and technically exact to achieve success. My crew was rowing precisely to the beat of my war drum, until I needed to push them off the boat to keep this ship moving forward.

That last run was always the hardest. Ten minutes of running is just five periods of two minutes of running. Now that I have one of those periods over, I'm one fifth of the way there. Two-fifths of the way there. It's halfway over at five minutes. Just a couple of more two-minute intervals after another minute. Anything to get that runner's high, whatever you have to tell yourself to persevere and complete the objective. The reward will be worth it in the end.

Commander's Log (Earth Year 4249): I know I made the correct decision to put everyone to sleep. All action is driven by human interest, they just weren't interested enough. Delayed gratification is the only way to get what is truly rewarding in life, they are shortsighted, only seeing instant satisfaction. Democracies have failed all throughout history, it's only been a matter of time everywhere it has been tried. Look at Rome and Athens. It's always been the case that the only way to move forward is to move toward a Monarchy. Look at Louis XIV of France and Augustus of Rome, this is the only way great progress can be made.

The two-party system featured in the United States was the perfect form of government to ensure that nothing ever got done. This would ultimately keep an overbearing government in check and limit the powers they had against their citizens. This was not a system that worked everywhere, and certainly not in this scenario I'm in right now. They'll all thank me in the end for making the correct power grab when we know they would all lead to a stalemate in decision making if given the opportunity.

Commander's Log (Earth Year 4517): I missed the tenth anniversary of Pluto revolving around our home star since its discovery while I was sleeping. At this point, it's looking like I'm going to be drifting through space until the end of the universe itself. How will it all end? The universe is expanding at an increasing rate but will gravity eventually win back the fight and create a big crunch? This could explain the creation of the big bang, a previous universe that crunched down to a single point and erupting into everything we know today. An endless cycle of universes expanding and collapsing in order to create the next universe. Which iteration of universes was this one? Or maybe the ever-increasing rate of expansion will cause all the atoms in the universe to be spaced too far apart in total entropy and create a big freeze.

Maybe the mysterious dark energy will have some kind of hand in our demise. Or maybe it's all a giant simulation and we're waiting for the programmer to unplug this matrix we're living in. Maybe I'll get to live long enough to see a Boltzmann brain or two pop into existence. Anything can happen when you're talking about the timetable of infinity that I'm dealing with. Who knows how it'll end. It's looking like I'm going to be here to experience it at this point.

Commander's Log (Earth Year 4989):

A Haiku:

Vast great dark abyss.
Black holes, pulsars, magnetars.
I've been led amiss.

Commander's Log (Earth Year 6346): I really should have just stayed on Earth. I was rich; I was a pretty decent looking guy. I decided not to get surgery for my male pattern baldness, which was such an easy fix. It was like getting a cavity filled and I had the best insurance money could buy, even though any policy covered that. I could have been a model or some kind of influencer if I had gotten plastic surgery like everyone else. I could have lived an easy life.

Here I am, floating through space on a mission like I'm some kind of savior for humanity. There's only one person who can save all of humanity from extinction, and I'm self-centered enough to think that it's me that is responsible for that purpose. I've spent my entire life thinking that I'm the only person fit for the job of solving every issue that has been placed in front of me. This is different.

Commander's Log (Earth Year 6823): My dreams have continued to get worse and worse as my journey through space has dragged on. Last night, I dreamed we had already landed on our new home and I awoke in the middle of the night and walked outside to gaze up at the night sky. I was admiring the nearest planet that just happened to be at its closest orbit to us at that very moment. I was thinking of the timelines and methods it would take to terraform the other planets and make it ready for another home, as I had once gazed at Mars with a similar adoration. I hoped that one day we would thrive to the point when we would separate and occupy both of the other worlds around the star, just like the need to diversify the human race had brought us here.

A meteor shower lit up the sky above me. It was like nothing I had ever seen on Earth. There were so many asteroids, it appeared there was one visible every second. They were just visible to the naked eye since there wasn't the same level of light pollution here as there was on Earth. I started realizing that some of these hunks of rocks were making it through the atmosphere and striking the ground. I yelled, "Everyone stay inside!" as I raced into the basecamp where the crew was just waking up.

Tinah asked, "We trusted you when you picked this planet. Did you not see the giant hunks of rocks that had littered the surface and wondered if there were more in a similar orbit?"

Just as I was about to defend myself, a massive object rattled the planet and sent objects flying all over the structure that we were taking shelter in. We looked out of the window in the distance to see a massive cloud of dust and soot heading up toward the atmosphere and blocking out any view of the sky.

Brad grabbed my face and yelled at me, "Didn't you learn from the dinosaurs not to pick a planet in the way of precarious drifting space rocks?"

Then I woke up. It was a very traumatic experience, and it doesn't seem to be getting any better. I've heard that if you write down your dreams when you wake up, you can control them. I'm hoping that I can quell these nightmares by writing them in my little diary here.

Commander's Log (Earth Year 7643): I pulled out the bottle of scotch at my last stop. It was not a good idea at all. Why did I bring that on the spacecraft with me? I had some very dark thoughts when I had enough of that in me. I always had a few rules on Earth about drinking, and one of them was to never drink alone. After all these years, I broke my rule when the stakes were the highest. At least all of it was gone now. I drank the rest of what I had. There was more down in long-term storage. I couldn't access that until we had reached our destination. I'm sober from here on out.

The hangover that always inevitably follows a night of drinking always outweighs the joy experienced the night before. I can never seem to remember this simple fact when I reach for the bottle. It turns out that putting yourself in cryo-sleep with a hangover does make the following wake-up process worse. No amount of sleep can get rid of that poison. Hopefully, writing this down in my space journal will be a reminder for me in the future to break this endless cycle of self-sabotage.

Commander's Log (Earth Year 8463):

A poem:

Traveling, traversing, transcending,
until andromeda collides with the milky way.
It seems to me, that his will be,
the guaranteed result of my stay.

Will I be spaghettified into a black hole?
That much, I do not know.
The only thing I can comprehend,
this mission has brought about my end.

I'm probably the best poet in the galaxy. The only poet alive in the galaxy.

Commander's Log (Earth Year 8928): I've experienced

an entire year since I've decided to not wake up the rest of the crew, an entire year of putting myself to sleep, waking myself up, following the wake-up procedures, and failing. Time and time again. Planet after planet after planet. Atmospheres stripped from planets, missing planets, not enough potential planets in a system here, too many planets on crash courses over there. Aliens everywhere, who would have thought the universe had so many separate occurrences of life forms?

Maybe I was too strict with my initial parameters for a solar system to move to. Maybe the perfect place just isn't out there. So far, only the Earth and one other system have intelligent life on it as far as we know, so maybe the universe really is just extremely hostile toward intelligent life as we know it. If there really is a perfect system, there will probably be intelligent life on it that won't want anything to do with us, like our other experience with life has shown us. Maybe I should just go back to one of the earlier not perfect systems we experienced in the trip and just settle. I should just get some sleep and move on to the next star.

Commander's Log (Earth Year 9006): I started eating dinner with the crew a few stops ago to feel a sense of normalcy. I didn't wake them up. I set everyone up with their favorite dishes and sat with them in the cryo-sleep room, having conversations with them about their favorite things from their files. I realized this was not a great use of resources as I had to make the decision to try to finish all of their dishes or waste them. The loneliness of my decision is really creeping in, like I've taken a long hike alone in the woods and my trail map has just been blown off into the wind.

What will I tell the crew when I finally wake them up? Will I act like we're on the very next planet, living a lie for the rest of my life when, in actuality, thousands of years have passed by on Earth. There's no way anyone would ever know. I can reset the clocks and everything on the ship. I'll just have to keep Karina from telling everyone. She must have some kind of reset or setting that will allow this. Is she really there or is she just a figment of my imagination? Karina, if you're reading this, flicker the lights twice. No light flickering, or maybe it's some sort of reverse psychology.

Commander's Log (Earth Year 9074): Where do we go when we die? It's always comforted me in knowing that there's nothing afterwards. Who would want to live forever? This has allowed me to make the most of my limited time I'm occupying in the universe, a small blip on the grand scale of cosmic time. But what if I'm wrong? What if there is such a thing as reincarnation as the Buddhists suggest? I can send myself out of the airlock and find out. Maybe this is my purgatory, waiting in a plane on a runway that may never take off to deliver me toward my final judgment. It's enough to make an atheist pray for judgment day.

Commander's Log (Earth Year 9268): I'm feeling lonely despite having my dear robot friend here to experience the repeated anguish of failure. There's an option I've been exploring in my head for some time now that I know I can't possibly consider. Should I wake up one of my crew members to share in this agony?

Brad had started the mutiny which led to my ultimate decision to place them all in this indefinite slumber. I can't possibly wake him up? Right? He seems to have a certain hunger for power like me, though. Maybe I can cut him a deal and keep him in a special place of power once we get to our new home.

Maybe Usha is who I can wake-up. A psychologist would certainly sympathize with my situation. This is the type of profession that could help the most in my current state and maybe assist in taming these nightmares. Who else would I need more in a situation such as this? The only risk in this choice would be her eventually playing some voodoo Jedi mind trick on me to admit we need the rest of the crew and a revival of the resistance that led to my current debacle. I've always heard growing up that the psychologists probing other people's disturbed minds often had worse things going on in their own brains. That can't be true, right?

Tinah perhaps? Her skills would obviously help me decide on a solar system to settle down in. This could put an end to my indecisiveness and persuade me to choose an endpoint for this seemingly rudderless ship. I really don't want to settle on anything less than perfection though, this might be the fate of humanity in our hands. We wouldn't want the future to rest on an imperfect solar system that would set us up for more failure like on Earth.

Maybe Justine? She can be the negative Nancy sometimes, though. I wonder if her parents thought about naming her Nancy. My parents had always told me that if I were a girl, they would have named me Rebecca. I wonder if Nancy's parents had a boy's name picked out for her as well. The universe may never know. I might need someone who is critical around me to keep me in check. But probably not.

Let's not make any rash decisions and sleep on this one.

Commander's Log (Earth Year 9589): There's really only two ways out of this at this point:

The first option is to set a course for the emptiest path of space I can imagine and just let the ship drift off into nothingness. If there is some divine power out there, they will certainly intervene to save the 254 other souls left that I have damned to an eternity of drifting through space. I'll just let Jesus take the wheel.

The only other option is to aim the ship back at Earth and hope that I was wrong all along and they figured out all the problems I believed were unsolvable. More than ten thousand years would have passed since we left the planet that humans have called home for thousands of years. What technological advancements would have been made since we were gone? Would anyone even remember or have records of who we are? Would humans have evolved since we've left? I'd be in big trouble if I chose this option, not even just a life of shame, but there would most likely be some legal repercussions. There might be no one left on the planet if some other extinction event took place. Maybe we will have the planet to ourselves.

Putting myself into hibernation at each stop and not knowing if I'm going to wake up on the other side is really taking its toll on my mental state.

I need to make a decision.

Chapter Nine

The Prime Mover
(Arbitrary Algorithm: Year 7348)

Today was the day. Isaac decided to wake himself up one day before the rest of the crew to get his head straight and his thoughts together. There was no turning back. Isaac had to act on the third day since everyone else was on their second day of waking up in almost total confusion. He didn't have to do any award-winning stuff, just enough for everyone to not look back at the day and be suspicious. Isaac was going to have to tell everyone what he did and there would be an all-out mutiny.

His loneliness would finally end. Isaac felt like he had traveled to the other side of the Earth alone and his airline had forgotten his luggage as he landed before midnight local time. It was like getting lost in an entirely new city after having a bunch of drinks, only to realize you didn't have your phone in your pocket because you left it somewhere you couldn't remember. Isaac imagined it was like he had been dropped in a foreign land where he didn't know the language spoken by anyone and there were no devices that would instantly translate in your ear for you.

None of those experiences could have actually compared to the despondency he had felt near the end of his time in solitary.

Isaac was reminded of a cenote he had swum in on one of his vacations to the Yucatan peninsula earlier in his life. He had descended into this chasm in the Earth twenty-five meters in depth, halfway filled with water. He was assured there was water at the bottom. When he reached the end of his descent on the ladder, there was no water at all. If he let go, he would just tumble down into the Earth for eternity. He had to reach his hand down to create ripples in the water to disrupt the sheet of glass he had been previously staring down at. Isaac felt like he did in that cenote except that there was no water at the bottom, and the rungs at the top of this ladder had disappeared.

Tarax Corporation had led them straight into a wormhole, with the promise that their new home would wait for them on the other side. Isaac was just realizing that there was no way to really know what was on the other end of this passage. The crew had been careening through time and space without the hope that they would ever be released from the wormhole's clutches.

Isaac figured he might as well look at the planet's data and imagery of this system while he was sitting around waiting for everyone to wake up and realize his demise.

"Karina, what do we have here?"

The screen in the command center displayed the data:

Jacobs-42
Distance (Light Years from Earth): 248.4
Apparent Magnitude: 8.91
Stellar Classification: G2V

Jacobs-42c
Mass: 0.91
Radius: 0.88
Period (Days): 326

Jacobs-42d
Mass: 1.05
Radius: 1.11
Period (Days): 418

Jacobs-42e
Mass: 1.18
Radius: 1.54
Period (Days): 526

Now he knew he was actually delusional. It was perfect. Three planets, one move-in ready and the other two weren't that far off, although he would want to confirm with Tinah. The star was very similar in size, classification, and remaining life to their dear and beloved Sol. The imagery made no indication that life had taken shape in any form on this system. Not too hot, not too cold, just right. Did he really just stumble upon the perfect Goldilocks zone? It had only taken a distance of 15,709,084 astronomical units away from Earth to get here.

The solar system featured breathtaking gas giants out in the distance that their children could look out at with their first telescopes. The sixth planet from the star made Isaac think of the first time he had gazed at Jupiter with his own eyes when he was a child. The many layers of storms on the planet gave him the comfort of the southern little layer cake his mom would always prepare for him when he was young. That was until he learned later about the scale of the winds on the giant storms that caused the storms that no human devices had ever survived. There was still a strange comfort about comparing them to the Twelve Apostles he had seen later in life along the great ocean road outside of Melbourne, Australia. The layers of limestone there had formed in the previous six thousand years before Isaac had witnessed them, about as long as he had been drifting through the galaxy.

Even a moon orbited the move-in ready planet with the perfect ratio of size to distance that would allow for total solar eclipses. Isaac could never forget the first time he had witnessed a solar eclipse. He had to plan it out far in advance to beat out the other junior astronomers that would flock to the path of totality when it was above land. It was always a disappointment to him when it was only above the ocean. The area where he had first witnessed the eclipse went from a sunny day to almost complete darkness in less than a minute. Streetlights turned on and the temperature felt like it dropped as the entire crowd around him cheered in amazement. It was the first time Isaac had cried in front of so many people and changed the trajectory of his entire life.

This day was an absolute miracle.

Isaac figured he could take a risk. He could put them all, including himself, back into a deep slumber and orbit around the planet for another few days and wake up with everyone else. This way, he wouldn't have to act and his grogginess would be real. He was almost certain they wouldn't remember these first two days after going back under, or even if they did, he could play it off as a ship malfunction. There's always the risk that he wouldn't remember to play along, though and confess to his terrible deeds before they all checked out the planetary data. It was too much of a risk to leave this up to his foggy third day brain.

"Karina, can you keep the fact that we have been traveling by ourselves for six thousand seven hundred and seventy-seven years a secret from the other crew members?" Isaac asked.

"I don't really know what a secret is. I'm only here to answer specific inquiries," Karina replied.

"Perfect, so as long as they don't ask you specifically what happened, I'll be alright?"

"It would be much easier if you just told them."

"So you do know the concept of a secret? You didn't see me check this star system out before everyone else woke up tomorrow, right?"

"Your secret is safe with me."

Isaac was in his bed late, thinking about the following

day. Now was when the real acting needed to take place. Isaac needed to act as if he was just waking up and playing along like normal, as if none of the last 6,777 years had ever taken place. His crew will feel sorry for ever having doubt and will never question his authority again. Isaac had about sixteen hours to perfect his lines and emotions before anyone else woke up. He could sleep in his comfortable quarters and then place himself in his cryo-chamber and wait for them all to emerge. It was perfect.

There was almost no way Isaac could be caught unless he slipped up and cracked. He had kept lies for his entire life, which he was at the midpoint of. Why not keep secrets for the second half of his life? He can set back all the time sensors on the ship and pretend like nothing happened. He would wipe all those silly diary entries that he was keeping to stay sane. No one will ever have to know what he had done.

He started thinking about his plan for the following day. Isaac had stumbled into the perfect scenario as he had many times in his rise to success on Earth, but he couldn't fall asleep as he continued to think about it. There was this deep aching in his gut that caused him to toss and turn. Everything was turning out right for Isaac after the dedication he put in by himself for all those centuries while the others slept peacefully. Something still wasn't right; however, it must be done. Maybe the sleep deprivation will add to the acting performance and keep everyone from knowing he had woken up before them. His exhaustion eventually won.

Isaac woke up to his alarm blaring in his quarters,

which was set to give him enough time to stumble into where the crew would eventually wake up on their third day. He didn't know exactly when everyone would wake up, so Isaac would lie in his chamber until at least one other person had awakened. He didn't want to give anyone room for suspicion that he had pulled some funny business before the others were fully aware. Isaac laid there with his eyes closed for what seemed like forever until Brad, the mutiny leader, had woken up first. Isaac heard him rise and rummage around for a few minutes before Isaac opened his eyes.

It was strange not to be met with Brad's cheery expression as he greeted Isaac. "You look rough, like you've aged as much as the ship has since the last stop. I guess your leadership role hanging in the balance really takes its toll."

"Leadership, in general, I suppose. I'm feeling good about this stop though. I'm thinking there'll be no need for any votes moving forward," Isaac replied.

"I thought about checking out the stats of this system and the suspense is killing me. I would much rather prefer that we all get to share in the experience of the beginning of your undoing."

"The more the merrier, I've always said."

The wake-up order followed the same sequence as previously established. Brad was usually first, followed by Tinah, Justine, then Usha. Isaac was always waking up in a different order depending on his dream sequences, or when he woke up early on purpose after waking up for years alone unknowingly to the crew. With everyone awake and alert, it was time for his performance to begin.

"Let's get this show on the road, Karina. Let's see what we got here," Brad said.

Brad was trying to keep this mutiny in full swing by taking charge. Isaac wanted to sit back and let someone else take the reins to not seem suspicious. Isaac tried to be as cool as a cucumber on the outside but he was nowhere near "easy peasy lemon squeezy" on the inside. He knew that just confessing would be the easiest option, but he didn't put in all of that effort alone for years just to have to confess his sins that quickly.

The screen in the command center displayed the data:

Jacobs-42
Distance (Light Years from Earth): 248.4
Apparent Magnitude: 8.91
Stellar Classification: G2V

Jacobs-42c
Mass: 0.91
Radius: 0.88
Period (Days): 326

Jacobs-42d
Mass: 1.05
Radius: 1.11
Period (Days): 418

Jacobs-42e

Mass: 1.18
Radius: 1.54
Period (Days): 526

Tinah's mouth was agape and remained that way for some time as she analyzed the stats displayed on the screen. "It's beautiful," she whispered.

The rest of the crew were unsure what they were looking at, though from Tinah's amazement, something was different about this location.

"It's perfect," Tinah rejoiced. "It's even better than our home solar system."

Brad's shoulders lowered, looking like a sad puppy with his tail between his legs. His weakened lust for power slowly turned to a look of amazement on his face as he realized that they were saved.

"I can't believe that we ever doubted you, Isaac. You knew that this system was out here all along, like you had envisioned this promised land in your dreams," Usha said in amazement.

So much for doctor-patient confidentiality, Isaac thought.

"I'll never question your authority again, for as long as we live on this new planet, you tell me to jump and I'll ask, how high?" Brad said before kissing Isaac right on the mouth.

That seemed like a little much. Who was Isaac to deny a little victory smooch?

"There's a magnetic field surrounding the planet that can shield us from the radiation from its star. I knew we were attracted to you like a magnet for a reason," Tinah said affectionately.

Isaac couldn't help but think about the terrible plot that he had unleashed without anyone's permission. If the crew had known he wielded that kind of power, they probably would have never left Earth.

"The first thing we do once we get down there is going to be erecting a statue of you," Justine proclaimed. "The person who gave humans a chance to continue among the cosmos."

The guilt was too much. Isaac finally cracked. He had to tell them everything. It was finally time to own up to all the terrible things he'd tried to get away with. He couldn't live this lie for the rest of his life with everyone, thinking he was some sort of God.

"Everything isn't exactly as it seems ..." Isaac's voice trailed off as he finished the statement.

"What do you mean? This star system meets all of your parameters. There's absolutely nothing I can find that would be a concern here," Tinah said with confidence.

"Everything with this solar system is perfect. How we got here, not so much. I had Tarax install an option on the ship to wake myself up and keep you all in hibernation. I've been traveling by myself and have experienced more than a year without you. Six thousand seven hundred and seventy-seven years of Earth time have passed since you all thought you were going to wake up from your last stop that you were aware of. I realize this end might not have justified the means, and it is completely understandable if you all will usurp my power or worse. However, I thought

I did what was best for the mission we embarked on long ago."

Every second of silence that passed after his admission of guilt was torturous. It felt like much longer, though, it was only ten or fifteen seconds until Justine finally interrupted the silence. "I feel completely violated since I didn't have a choice in this decision."

"I'm so sorry," Isaac replied.

Justine added, "But we have also finally made it to paradise."

Brad would certainly have to make his opinion known. "What do you mean? Forget about paradise. I'll never be alright with what you've done. We went from voting on our fate to a complete autocracy without us having any say in the matter."

"We have been brought to the promised land, though," Tinah added.

"You can issue justice and jail me if you'd like once we get down to the surface," Isaac said and held out his wrists, offering them to be cuffed. "I would completely understand."

"There's no need for all that. We still need a leader who can make tough decisions, and I still think you're the person for that role. No more tricks though, everyone has a say in any decisions going forward," Brad declared.

"Agreed." Isaac retracted his wrists and held his hands up. "I don't have any more tricks up my sleeve. Complete transparency on the new planet."

He had meant every word he said after revealing the

selfish actions he had taken and planned to be a completely changed person at their new home. This would be a new beginning for him and a new chapter in their journey for everyone who had shared this completely humbling experience with him. They would create a society that always looked up toward the stars and continued the progress and innovation of mankind. Their new society would never return to the complacency that had gotten them into this mess. They all couldn't wait to see what new adventures awaited them in their new home.

Once the spacecraft landed, it was designed to fold out in all directions in order to provide some additional immediate functions.

There was a large 3-D printing section that would provide them with all the different parts and objects that the ship wasn't large enough to carry. This also included a mining and refining area that would provide them with the initial materials from the regolith of the new terrain to print objects with. They were still unsure of the materials that they could draw out of a potential planet, and this would provide them a solid foundation for expanding their research.

There was a small lab that folded out that would serve as the beginning of their meat cultivation. Plants were very important, but there would also be a need for protein in the long run. The animal muscle cells they brought with them would provide them with all the chicken, beef, and pork that they would ever need. All of this with much less carbon emissions than traditional methods that humans on Earth just couldn't break themselves away from. Calling it "lab-grown meat" was always the hurdle that most people couldn't get over on Earth. Since there are no animals being brought with them, the only meat available would be "cultivated meat" and that's what they would call it henceforth. The crew was all exuberant to try it out six weeks after landing since they were limited to the five options available to them along the way there.

A small hydroponics greenhouse would fold out from the ship in another direction that would initiate a new supply of nutritional crops necessary for sustained population growth. One of the first orders of business would set up an additional greenhouse where they would start growing their harvest size. This would get them started though. The food they brought wouldn't last forever with a population that would soon be awakened after landing and hopefully multiplying; they would need a steady future supply of nutrients. There wasn't enough room in the spacecraft to bring soil from Earth and they wouldn't be able to trust an extraterrestrial soil immediately, so hydroponics would be needed.

An important step would lie out the footprint of where all their infrastructure would reside. Setting up solar fields that would provide electricity was vital for everything they would do for success on their new planet. The ship would arrive already featuring a nuclear fusion power reactor, kind of like how they use on aircraft carriers on Earth way back in the day. That would only be a short-term solution. A strong solar presence would be vital in preserving their new atmosphere as they were not carefully doing back on their home world. The area needed to be large enough to plan for plenty of future growth but not so large that it would obstruct the ability to set up other key elements of their infrastructure. It also had to be close enough for voltage drop not to undermine their efforts. A delicate equilibrium.

After the tension settled down, the crew gathered near the spacecraft window and gazed down at their new world in complete awe. The area they had selected to set up their base camp reminded Isaac of the Aburrá Valley when he visited Medellín, the city of eternal Spring, in Colombia. There were two large mountainous regions that surrounded the area which provided a stable climate for their new civilization. Isaac thought about how this must have been the same feeling when the first Martians explored Valles Marineris on Mars.

The river separating these two regions might provide a source of drinkable water and even hydro generation for the colony. There was also an ocean that could have potential for marine life near their new base camp to the north. Oceans covered 64 percent of the surface of their new home compared to the 71 percent ocean-covered Earth.

"I spent all that time by myself with my thoughts and I couldn't come up with a name for our new planet. I finally have it. We're going to name it Alernus," Isaac declared as they were descending into the passenger section of the spacecraft.

Tinah was staring at Isaac with a perplexed look, hoping that he would get the hint and figure out that he needed to handle things as a group after his stunt on their journey.

"But that's just my thought. We can put it up for a vote. Any suggestions?"

"I don't think it looks like an Alernus," Justine replied.

"How about New Earth?" suggested Brad.

"I didn't come all this way for such an absurd and boring name like that," Tinah retorted.

"New Luna, New Sol. I can keep going."

"Please don't," Justine said.

"It's tough when all the celestial bodies back home have already claimed all the good sounding Roman and Greek deities," Tinah said.

"Usha, any ideas?" asked Isaac.

"How about Cardea? There were a bunch of celestial bodies back home named after gods. What about the goddesses? She was the goddess of the hinge and protected the family and the fate of humanity is really hinged on this planet right now," said Usha.

Everyone pondered the new name and couldn't find any objections. "That has a nice ring to it," Tinah finally said.

"And our new beautiful moon can be Carna. She provides us with strength."

"Usha, those are solid. Any ideas for naming our star?" Isaac asked.

"How about Vacuna? The goddess of rest after a harvest. I think we could all use a rest after what we've all been through."

"All in favor?" Isaac said as he looked around the room with everyone nodding in agreement. He was really embracing democracy.

Humanity had survived for so many generations, despite the cornucopia of threats that had tried to stamp them out over multiple millennia. Life can seem so fragile when looking at each individual and even when considering they had been limited to a single solar system, and at one time, a single planet. Many of the best political and economic systems in place over the years had always been successful due to the individual looking out for what was best for themselves. All of life had always survived throughout time as a result of every living thing doing what was best for their own survival.

Isaac and his crew had ventured out across the galaxy, against all odds, and stuck to his parameters against the staggeringly overwhelming odds against them.

Chapter Ten

The Engineer
(Cardea: Year 1)

The overview effect around this planet would differ slightly from the feelings that were provoked when Brad had been hovering above the Earth. There would be a whole new appreciation for the completely untouched terrain of this extraterrestrial body. So much opportunity awaited them down below and they would need to do things differently from the start to avoid another scenario like Earth. When hovering above the Earth, there was a feeling that you had to go back down and convince everyone to change their ways to right all the wrongs committed while abusing the planet for many years. Here, there was an eagerness to get down to the planet and implement ways they could preserve this pristine landscape.

There was no reason to wake up all the passengers before reentry just to experience a fiery death. Although catastrophe was not the plan, it was still a possibility.

The crew needed to head down to where their passengers were and have a little more zero-gravity fun before the next perilous part of their journey. It felt strange for Brad every time he climbed down the ladder that led to the center of the spacecraft. He was used to following the rule of using three points of contact when climbing ladders, except in this case he wouldn't need to since gravity would be taken away as he approached the bottom. Brad felt like an interstellar firefighter as he squeezed the ladder edges to slow himself down as he reached the destination instead of landing on a nonexistent floor.

Brad hadn't met most of the people who had been in storage this whole time, however, he did read most of their files along the trip and he couldn't help keeping them in his mind as he plummeted downward through the atmosphere. He couldn't wait for them all to see the planet they'd selected. The nonrotating section of the spacecraft would detach from where the crew had been living for the duration of the trip when it was time to head down to the planet. The rotating section of the ship would remain in orbit and break off into sections providing GPS and other various satellite features, like climate and environmental monitoring.

Just as no experience on Earth's surface could prepare an individual for reaching the speed required to leave the influence of its gravity, there's absolutely no experience that compares to the terror of entering a planet's atmosphere. As the gravity of the planet pulls down at an ever-increasing attraction toward the ground, the particles of air cause friction and do everything in their power to tear a spacecraft to shreds. This does a great job in slowing objects down before slamming into the ground at an insane speed, but there's also the risk of being eviscerated.

The hot plasma that forms around a descent vehicle is a blistering 1,600 degrees Celsius and obstructs the view outside of the windows. There is a blackout period of four minutes where the crew won't be able to communicate with anyone outside of this vessel, not that there's anyone else still in existence to communicate with that they knew of.

Once they made it through the scariest four minutes, which would seem longer than the entire trip through the galaxy, light would finally make its way back through the windows. They would still travel at a ridiculous speed and hear the release of the large parachutes to decrease their speed even further into a manageable landing. Brad knew exactly how long they took to open. Every passing second would make him less sure that he'd remembered correctly. Finally, they would all be thrown into their seatbelts, strapping them into their seats and signifying the successful deployment of the chutes.

They would still travel at a speed that could seriously injure them during touchdown at the preselected landing area. Within the last few seconds of their descent, reverse thrusters should gently settle them down onto the new ground. Just as Tarax promised them thousands of years ago, they would have made it to their new world.

It had taken much longer to find their new home than they originally planned; the resources on the spacecraft were depleted from Isaac's solo journey. Not enough shelter would be immediately provided for all of their passengers, either. Some preparations needed to take place by the original crew. They had achieved the main mission of finding a new planet and now the real work began. The spacecraft itself would serve as the crew's initial shelter and also be the center from which all of their operations would expand from. It was outfitted with a small medical bay that could deal with most minor emergencies until a more adequate medical building could be established.

The first shelters would be small and would likely house more people than most folks would be comfortable with. It would be necessary to unfreeze additional workers to complete additional tasks to grow their society. They couldn't wait until they would be completely comfortable in their housing situation, or they would never make the progress. This wasn't about comfort in the early stages of creating a foundation for society. They had to put in the grunt work at this point to ensure success of the mission in the long run.

The crew needed to be selective when they decided who to wake up and at what time to wake them up. One of the first citizens they woke up was Dr. Jamal Williams. He was their back-up physician in case something happened to Raul. It was important to not wait until an emergency had struck before waking him up since they had known very well, from personal experience, that it would take three or four days before he would be productive after thousands of years in hibernation. Dr. Williams could provide a certain extent of help in mundane tasks in the early building of society. Regardless, he was necessary to be around and available in case disaster struck.

Three days had gone by in their new home and their mini civilization was taking shape. The beginning of their barracks was being erected and the constant buzzing of the mining and 3-D printer were blending in with their surroundings as sensory adaptation took full effect. The crew was outside of the Arbitrary Algorithm, doing various activities to get their new colony prepared for their passengers.

A strange voice coming from the ship was just discernible over the noise.

"Where? Where am I?"

Brad spun around, taking notice of their new guest. "Welcome to your new home, Dr. Williams!"

"The robot lady filled me in a little, but all the puzzle pieces still aren't fitting into place."

"We have been in your shoes many times over on our long journey here. We know exactly how you feel. Especially Isaac. You'll have to ask him about that."

"So, we didn't die? We actually made it?"

"That's right, we finally made it to Cardea. Isn't it beautiful?"

"It kind of looks like Earth."

"Same-same, but different. I'm glad you have finally woken up because Isaac wouldn't let me take the rover anywhere to explore our new lands. He said it would be too dangerous without a physician around."

"Glad I could help. I would love to take a ride with you sometime."

"Not so fast," Isaac interjected. "We need to keep you safe in case anything happens to us. Unfortunately, we're going to need you to stick around camp on light duty."

"Didn't the other ship have a physician in their crew?" Dr. Williams asked.

"The other ship didn't make the perilous journey through space," Isaac answered.

"Yet," Usha added.

"They could still be out there on their way to this planet. For the time being, Dr. Williams, you will be our head physician on Cardea. We need to keep you safe," Isaac said.

"Understood, and my condolences for the potential loss of your other crew members."

"The shelters are taking shape and we're going to wake up the others as our food supplies are bolstered."

"These shelters are rough. They remind me of some of my sleeping situations when I was a resident physician working twenty-four-hour shifts back on Earth."

"We're not going to have you just sitting around though. You're going to be on the welcoming committee for every new passenger we unthaw. It has been a while since we had our first cryo-sleep waking experience, so you're perfect for the job. Initially, I wanted to have all the satisfaction of welcoming our passengers and to have their unending gratitude for myself, but it is important that this is a team effort where everyone contributes."

"I'm glad I'll be putting all those years of schooling to good work."

The colonists would still revel at Isaac whenever they

were in his presence, but he took more of a backseat approach with most operations to give the crew more credit for the work they were doing. The crew woke their passengers up in intervals of five every day from that point on to not overwhelm their resources and give them all a proper welcome to their new paradise. The first of the civilians to be woken up was a small crew of engineers and technicians to assist Brad in planning and constructing the infrastructure. There was a diverse schedule of professions afterward, including farmers, fishers, biologists, cooks, sustainability experts, and various other scientists and medical professionals.

On day fifty-six on Cardea, Isaac gathered everyone in front of the opening of the Arbitrary Algorithm for the unveiling of the first pairings of procreation partners to take place.

Brad purposefully positioned himself near Justine and gave her a nudge and said, “Here’s the moment we’ve all been waiting for. Time to seal our destiny.”

Justine rolled her eyes and replied, “Don’t worry, as the computer scientist, I snuck into the script of the program and added a statement ensuring that we couldn’t get paired up.”

“I know you wouldn’t sabotage our fate like that. We’ll just see how the chips fall.”

Isaac interrupted all the side conversations and googly eyes being exchanged by the potential mates and opened the meeting by saying, “Welcome, everyone. This is the first of what will likely be an annual process to determine how we will grow our population. There are strict rules that need to be abided by since we lost half of our gene pool on the way here. We didn't want it to work like this, but we all agreed before we left Earth that we might need to do this if something catastrophic were to happen to one of the spacecrafts on the way. Our ship's AI, Karina, who most of you have met, has rerun the combinations based on our new availability and these decisions are final. I, nor anyone else, have seen what Karina has picked, so that there has been no funny business. I cannot decide who I'm paired with. Karina, show us on the big screen what we have."

Brad frantically searched for his name like he had just ran down to the auditorium doors of his high school to find out what character he was playing in the musical.

"No, freaking, way," Justine slowly said.

"I can't find myself. Are you mad you're not with me?" Brad said as his eyes still scrolled through the list. "Oh, there it is, jackpot."

Later that day, everyone turned in for the night; some folks paired off to get a head start on their civic duty assigned to them. Others were more cautious, tracking their cycles and making sure they put forth the minimal physical activity involved.

Brad saw Justine heading back to her abode, and she waved him over seductively. It wasn't what it seemed. It was another trick she was playing on him. He expeditiously walked over just in case it wasn't though.

He entered her dwelling and said, "I know this isn't what you wanted after traveling all this way across the galaxy, so I can go ahead and get your sample ready, and you can do what you want with it."

Justine didn't say anything and walked over to the door and slowly closed it. Once they had some privacy, she whispered, "There's only one way I want this to happen, and it's not the artificial way."

Justine reached up and grabbed a handful of his hair from the back of his head, pecking small kisses along his neck until she made her way across his right cheek, and finally to his lips. She effortlessly brought Brad closer to her as he melted into her embrace like he had always dreamed of. She maneuvered him to her bed as the kissing grew more intense until she ravenously threw him onto the bed and undressed. Brad wondered if this had been lurking under the surface for the entire trip or if some magic was created when Karina made her decisions earlier that day. He didn't care either way. He was just happy to be along for the ride.

Brad woke up in a panic the next morning, alone, in a different room than the one he had been staying in since they arrived at their new planet. *Did the events of last night truly happen or was this sadly a figment of my imagination? Or was the entire day and Karina's ceremony all made up?* The door of his new environment opened; he quickly covered his bare body to avoid revealing too much to this mystery person. Shockingly, it turned out to be Justine.

"Morning," Justine said as she walked in with two cups of coffee in her hands. "Do you always sleep this late? Or just after mediocre performances like last night?"

Mediocre? So, it did happen. It's a miracle. Wait, mediocre?

Justine continued, "I'm just messing with you. I really didn't have any expectations going in, but I have to say, good work."

"Thanks," Brad said reluctantly. "I'm still not sure what to think."

"I'm not going to lie; I was pretty devastated when Karina made her decisions. I thought this was all some sick joke and then it slowly transformed throughout the day into a why not kind of feeling. I'm not trying to get your hopes up, who knows?"

"Who knows? That's the best news I've heard in almost seven thousand years. I can't wait to tell Isaac."

"Yeah, no. Can you just keep this on the down low for now? I'm not sure if this euphoria will fade."

"I promise."

That evening, the original crew sat at their original dinner table inside the ship; another makeshift table was set up for some of their freshly thawed out guests. The original crew had dinner together a few times a week, and they always included their recently awakened guests to make them feel welcomed. It felt like they were back on Earth celebrating Thanksgiving and they had all their new crew members sitting at the kiddie table. Plus, with all the new food offerings they were trying out, this was even better than Thanksgiving. Instead of turkey, they were serving the meats they had grown themselves.

It was Brad's turn to say grace. It was never really a prayer that anyone would open with, more of an airing of grievances.

Brad opened up the conversation and said, "This feels like Thanksgiving. I always hated Thanksgiving."

"Here we go," said Justine.

"The forced family fun time would make me anxious for weeks out," Brad continued, not acknowledging Justine, "that's why I mostly traveled outside of the country during Thanksgiving. Whenever I was home, I would always fill my plate with mashed potatoes and stuffing smothered in gravy. Turkey just kind of sucks. Luckily, we have these delicious lab-grown meats to make this not suck like Thanksgiving,"

Brad paused and stuck a fork into a hunk of pork and jammed it into his mouth.

"Cultivated meat," Isaac interjected.

"Yeah that, this isn't too bad!" Brad exclaimed with a mouth full of food.

After dinner concluded, Brad strolled into Isaac's makeshift office with a determination that caught Isaac by surprise.

"You look like a man on a mission. This ought to be good. Wait, I noticed that smile you had on at the dinner table whenever Justine interrupted you. You and Justine? Direct donation? Not artificial insemination?" Isaac asked.

"It. Was. Magical." Brad couldn't keep it to himself, even though he had promised Justine he would keep his mouth shut. "I didn't tell you that. No one can know. I've got a good thing going here and I can't ruin it."

"Congrats, your secret is safe with me. Was there something else you wanted to bring to my attention?"

"Captain, I haven't been drunk for over seven thousand years," Brad continued. "I don't think I've ever been dry for that long. I think it's time to reward myself."

"I did hide a couple bottles of scotch in storage for us once we got here. I'm thinking we're going to need a long-term solution for this quandary, though."

"I used to home brew beer and wine a little back on Earth when everything would come in a nice little pre-measured kit. It always tasted better than commercial products, knowing it came from the fruits of your own labor."

"I'm thinking we're not going to be able to get any kits like that shipped out here. The shipping fees from Earth would be astronomical too."

"When I was making wine, it was pretty simple. We're just going to need a fermentation vessel, sugar from some source, and yeast to break the sugar down into alcohol."

"So, we're going to make some toilet bowl moonshine?"

"More like bathtub moonshine. And we can just let whatever yeast is in the air ferment it. It most likely won't taste great. It will be booze though."

"Beautiful. It would be pretty reckless to use our precious resources for this. We can start a small batch eventually and see how it goes once we have more farming going."

"I've even thought of the name for our distillery …"

"You've really been thinking about this a little too much."

"Good hooch, made from scratch. Good Scratch!"

"That's actually pretty solid."

"I'm good at something every once in a while."

"Even a broken clock is correct twice a day, I suppose."

Everything was going perfectly with the solar array setup until complacency led to their first major accident at their new home. A technician working under Brad hadn't realized that a connection that led from the solar array back into the general grid of the colony wasn't de-energized until it was too late. Brad was having a conversation with the technician when he had stopped replying in mid conversation. Brad was already short-handed with folks skilled in the trades. He was devastated to hear that a death had happened under his watch while his mind was drifting off in conversation about women and booze. The downfall of many great men throughout history.

The original crew were all gathered around the grave site as they made their final respects to the first citizen of their new home that would become one with the regolith.

"We all knew that there would be many dangers that came with settling down on a new planet. Not only the unexpected strife that would come with exploring new lands, there were also the known dangers that are always lurking around every corner," Isaac said.

Brad knew he was mostly trying to console him and replied, "I didn't think it would happen this quick, and as a result of the work I'm in charge of."

"This can all really be chalked up to being my fault. I'm the one that led everyone on this crazy adventure."

"Everything on the way was your fault, but this one is on me, commander."

Brad knew his joke was just a defense mechanism in order to stop thinking about the matter at hand. Brad was enraptured when he was given control over the various engineering projects, but he hadn't been aware of the potential burdens that came along with leadership. He thought about the crew of the Recursive Singularity and how Isaac was responsible for more destruction than he had been on this day. He felt dejected because Isaac had been solely over encumbered with the affliction of being responsible for the fate of the other crew for all this time. It seemed as everyone standing around the grave site in silence thought about the other crew of five and their passengers who had never arrived at their destination.

Chapter Eleven

The Environmental Scientist (Recursive Singularity: Year 7358)

The crew of the Recursive Singularity was on their eleventh stop when they took a vote to place Raul and Stephanie in an indefinite cryo-sleep to conserve resources. Victoria could wake them back up if needed, however, Victoria, Amy, and James were more essential to the mission at hand. Victoria the commander, Amy the biologist, and James the psychologist.

They were measuring by the number of stops since the internal clocks on the ship had shut down. However long they were sedentary in space, was long enough to be too far away from the Arbitrary Algorithm to maintain communications. Their spaceship was accelerating to 5 percent of the speed of light after their stop at the Bolden-121 dual star system when their momentum halted. The crew had no way to tell how long they had been sitting stagnant in the empty void in space.

They settled with the fact they may never see the other crew again. Victoria and her crew followed the predetermined path laid out in Isaac's plan and still had not found a potential world. They had not run into the Arbitrary Algorithm or its remnants, which gave them hope they would run into them at their new home at some point.

Victoria thought about the crew of the other ship on their journey. She had plenty of time to reread their files and wondered if they had put a couple people back into cryo-sleep just as their crew had long ago. Who would they pick? Isaac would most likely choose to put their engineer into a deep sleep like they had. Brad would most likely argue with them all the way into his sleep chamber. Justine would most likely be their other person. Victoria and crew were living proof that the ship's computers can malfunction, and it wouldn't have been any help if the computer scientist onboard was in a deep sleep, anyway. Like Brad, they could wake her up if needed.

It was hysterical for Victoria to think that Brad and Justine would be the two individuals that would be placed down to rest with each other for what could be the rest of their entire existence. Justine was probably pissed. They probably had to put her in hibernation first, so she wouldn't know Brad would join her.

Her crew took turns comforting whichever crew member was having doubts at every stop. Victoria knew that the other crew would keep their psychologist awake since it had been an integral part of keeping their crew sane along the way. She couldn't imagine what it would be like without them there. They had run into star systems with planets that had disappeared, a bunch of planets that were inhospitable to human life, unintelligent alien species, and every other scenario imagined. Victoria wondered how the other crew analyzed the alien life of each planet they came across and hoped they took an abundance of caution in Amy's absence. They persevered and stuck to Isaac's original requirements for a new home.

Victoria uttered the phrase that she had said many times before, "Karina, what do we have here?"

The screen in the command center displayed the data:

Jacobs-42
Distance (Light Years from Earth): 248.4
Apparent Magnitude: 8.91
Stellar Classification: G2V

Jacobs-42c
Mass: 0.91
Radius: 0.88
Period (Days): 326

Jacobs-42d
Mass: 1.05
Radius: 1.11
Period (Days): 418

Jacobs-42e
Mass: 1.18
Radius: 1.54

Period (Days): 526

"All right, I'm starting to feel like an expert and this system is perfect. There's no way Isaac would have passed this one up," said Victoria.

Amy nodded in agreement. She said, "I hate to say it. If Isaac isn't here, I would have to suggest that we're going to have to settle down here and stop searching for him."

"I think we're all in agreement. We can continue to hope that they're still out there. It just isn't worth it to continue to risk our lives. This looks like paradise," said James.

"Let's look at the imagery of the planet to see if there's life and to scan for a potential place to set up shop," said Victoria.

The crew scanned the imagery together until James made a discovery. "There's a perfect spot here. Unfortunately, it looks like another intelligent alien species might already have established themselves on this planet. I knew it was too good to be true."

Victoria thought about all the amazing aspects of their new society that could be a reality if they landed on this planet. Waking up their passengers, exploring the terrain, and having beautiful children to keep their existence going for millennia to come. She wondered if they would ever experience these magnificent joys of life on another planet.

She pondered negative scenarios that would eventually arise, like the first crime committed in a new society.

A society had never existed where all members contributed the same amount as everyone else, which eventually led to the never-ending struggle between the haves and the have nots. Someone would probably hoard food for themselves or commit some act of violence, causing them to debate a system of justice.

Their psychologist, James, could be the purveyor of truth and settle all justice. He would know all the gossip of every individual. People would probably be reluctant to tell him things in therapy sessions, though. They certainly wouldn't want to decide only among the original crew, which could create an oppressive caste system that never worked out well in the end. Victoria didn't want some sort of *Animal Farm* situation arising. They would most likely end up settling things like they did back on Earth with a jury of their citizens who would decide their fate.

These thoughts were worthless until they found their forever home.

"Maybe we can overtake this species and claim this world as our own?" James questioned.

Amy stood up and grabbed James' arm and slowly whispered, "It can't be …"

"I know. We probably shouldn't go down this road again. Yet again, disappointment," replied James.

"It is!" Amy exclaimed as she jumped up and down. "It's Isaac!"

They all rose to their feet and embraced each other, rotating around in a circle and jumping up and down.

"Karina," Victoria said when she could finally speak

through her tears of excitement, "can you open up communications with the Arbitrary Algorithm base station down on the planet?"

"You're connected."

"Isaac, is it really you?" Victoria said.

"I recognize that voice. There's no way. After all these years, Victoria?" Isaac replied.

"We never doubted for a second that we would catch up with y'all! Okay, maybe for a few seconds."

"We were all terrified when we first saw that new object floating around in the sky heading toward us. I know exactly how that first intelligent species we encountered thousands of years ago felt now. I can't believe this. Come on down whenever you're ready! There's another location about five kilometers from here that would be perfect to start our second base location."

"We'll see you soon, good buddy!"

The outer door of the Recursive Singularity lowered as a rover pulled up containing the original five members of Isaac's crew. Isaac popped out of the driver's side door, walked over to the entrance of the Recursive Singularity, and welcomed Victoria's embrace. Everyone else naturally paired up with another member of the other crew and hugged until everyone welcomed each member separately. Isaac's crew looked older than when they had last seen them. Additional wrinkles had added to their faces and even some gray hairs were noticeable.

"Welcome to year ten on Cardea! You're ten years too tardy for the party," Isaac said.

"Cardea, I like that. Year ten, I don't know how I feel about that," Victoria said.

"Did you see our moon, Carna? Don't stare directly at Vacuna."

They piled into the rover and Isaac gave them the updates of their society as he drove them back to the base camp of the Arbitrary Algorithm. To everyone's surprise, the first baby born was a product of a couple members of the original crew, Justine and Brad. Karina swore up and down that she did not pick them on purpose. It was just how the genetic model simulated the best possible outcome for multigenerational success out of the remaining 255 people. Their beautiful girl was born just eleven months after they had initially landed on the planet. Justine and Brad didn't waste much time, strictly business. Until they made their marriage official a few months later.

Once the crew gathered in front of the original Arbitrary Algorithm base camp landing site, Isaac showed off all that they had accomplished in their time on the planet. The population had grown to 1,178 citizens in their ten years on the planet. The initial passengers were nearing the age of not reproducing anymore, so the new group of citizens would need to reproduce in an arranged fashion, just as the initial colony had. These unique family structures would provide an endless amount of work for a family therapist. Everyone in their new settlement would be required to participate in biweekly sessions to ensure the breeding codes were strictly followed, regardless of relationship status. It would still be a couple of generations before there weren't any restrictions on who could produce with whom, but they were making great progress and reinforcements had just arrived.

There was a large school building which was more of a babysitting operation, since there were many more children than adults in society. Most of their schooling would consist of on-the-job training, learning the operations it takes to grow their society since the original members were getting too old for physical work.

There was a question that was burning in the back of Victoria's mind and she didn't want to seem too eager with other matters being discussed. When there was a little pause in the conversation, she finally asked, "What was contained in the first message you sent back to Earth? And have you received anything from them yet?"

The other crew traded glances as if everyone were waiting for the next person to be the bearer of bad news.

Brad finally answered, "We thought it was best to not send a message to Earth."

Amy reframed the question; she could not comprehend that answer. "You never sent any messages to Earth? Have they sent any messages here?"

Isaac elaborated, "We have not received any attempts of contact from Earth. We knew we would most likely never hear from them again after being knocked off course early in our trip. We were so far off of our initial itinerary timeline that they most likely would miss communicating with us at every location afterwards, and were assuming there isn't anyone left on the planet, since none of our messages were ever returned along the way."

"Earth not responding along the way is no excuse for you to not try to attempt to communicate with them once you got here. You have had ten years here that you could have been sending signals to Earth," Amy added.

"They wouldn't even get one of our messages for another two hundred forty years if we sent one, anyway. What is the use?" Brad asked rhetorically.

"There could still be people on Earth that are trying to crawl their way out of an extinction and you could provide them a haven," pleaded Amy.

"We had a lot of discussion about this when we first got here and it always seems to pop up in conversation at various points in the last decade. We always return to the experience we had with our first intelligent species that we encountered when we started our journey into the galaxy. We agree with them. It is most likely best that we don't ruin what we have here and leave everything that was in the past where it belongs, on Earth," Isaac explained.

Almost interrupting Isaac, Brad added, "And we plan on keeping it that way."

"I can't believe you all agreed to this," said Amy.

"When we landed, we decided we would take a vote on all decisions going forward. This is what most of society agreed on, and I don't think your ship will overthrow the majority. We can discuss this further down the road once you and your passengers are more integrated with our society. That is the situation as it stands," Isaac said.

Victoria walked with Isaac to the Arbitrary Algorithm

to speak in private.

"This is impressive what you have done with your colony. I can only hope to have the same success with the passengers I have brought along," Victoria said.

"That is actually what I wanted to talk to you about. We have plenty of lessons learned and advice we can give to get everyone started and assimilated into our already growing community. I would like to lead in the efforts," Isaac said.

"That is a lot to handle on top of your responsibilities here, don't you think?"

"There is a great team around me here that does most of the work. I just guide everyone in the right direction. It's time for change around here. We need someone with fresh ideas to take over and to provide a fresh perspective on how to prevent another Earth debacle."

"Who are you going to appoint?"

"I'm appointing you, Victoria. It will be a slow transfer of power, but you will eventually take over completely."

"I thought that was where you were going with this conversation, but I didn't want to get ahead of my skis. Why not Brad? Or Usha? They might feel a little betrayed that I'm coming in and seizing power on my first day."

"They'll understand. We have plenty of checks and balances in place to restrict the potential for a hostile takeover by anyone, and you were more qualified to be the commander of this mission than I ever was. I just had the money to make it a possibility."

"I don't know what to say."

"Say that you accept my offer."

"I accept."

Victoria's crew had to adjust to the already established society. Having a colony move-in ready, however, was a situation they wouldn't trade for anything after their years in space. They had escaped their stagnant fates on Earth and traded it in for a wondrous expedition across the galaxy that led them to a hopeful future that they all believed in.

It was up to Victoria to make sure that what happened on Earth would never become the fate of the many generations to come on Cardea. The latest crew would create another town centered around their spacecraft that had just touched down. They would still need to work extremely closely with the original colony in order to join as one, eventually. They needed to ensure that they would shield themselves from the dangers of separate contentious societies that had led to destruction on Earth.

Epilogue

The Original Commander (Cardea: Year 39)

A few years had passed on Cardea, and both the original crews, who guided the maiden voyage, showed that time had indeed passed. There was a time when they would be out in the unknown, driving the rovers around to explore new corners of their new home. That time was a distant memory at this point.

Their population was at 5,267 and many of the reproduction restrictions had been lifted. However, breeding wasn't entirely open. When two people who were romantically involved wanted to have children, they would need to consult Karina in order to make sure they had the blessing of genetic viability to keep their posterity thriving.

Good Scratch distillery was making plenty of products and was even tasting decent since the early days of experimentation with Brad and Isaac. The white lightning bathtub moonshine they had started from had eventually transformed into a botanical gin, a smooth vodka, and a sweet bourbon-like whiskey. All of this was crafted from the barley and potatoes grown to adapt to the foreign topsoil of their new planet they resided on. Victoria was taken aback by the progress they had made, from barely being able to ration their hydroponic vegetable supply for their growing population to having the abundance for experimenting with great tasting libations.

Victoria read over the daily briefing provided to her by her assistant. She looked through the update at the pictures of the newest generation of daredevils utilizing the terrain for all sorts of new extreme sporting adventures. Victoria wondered why citizens resorted to unthinkable ways to damage their bodies, as if there wasn't enough work to keep them occupied. Her own children had led the charge in finding a section of the river farther inland from their initial base camp that provided death defying currents she experienced on New Zealand's Rangitata River on Earth. Victoria would definitely join in if her aging body would allow her to.

The younger civilians in society were even free climbing the cliff sides that contained their main city on each side. They already had the means of visiting the other sides of these mountains with their drones, but that wouldn't stop the younger generations from needing to see this new land with their own eyes. Much like Victoria buying her own telescope when she was younger to gaze out into the universe with her own eyes instead of relying on images from expensive earth-based and space telescopes. It was just a memory for Victoria to think about herself, summiting the mountain that were the interstellar spaces in between potential worlds on the journey that brought her to this land.

Although terraforming efforts hadn't started yet, they were being discussed for the other planets. Their jet propulsion lab was just being developed and they would soon start sending robots off to the other two planets to begin those efforts. This is exactly how the process had begun on Mars and Victoria knew they had to put rules in place to not allow for the same stagnation of progress that resulted from those efforts. Victoria let her mind drift on what had ever become of their originating solar system.

Victoria's assistant knocked on the slightly ajar door and said, "There's an urgent message that you need to be aware of."

"What could be so important at this hour?" Victoria asked.

"You won't believe me unless I show you."

"Alright, let's see this super important message."

Victoria grabbed the tablet and read the message:

"Jacobs-42, this is Sam Larkin, the prime-leader of Earth. We have developed space telescopes far superior to previous models that allow us to see the exact compositions of atmospheres in distant exoplanets. We have discovered that the Jacobs-42 system features the perfect world to spread the footprint of humanity to. We are sending this broadcast out ahead of time to notify any potential survivors of the Tarax space missions that we are on our way with crews to occupy the new planet. Please confirm if there are any survivors."

Victoria read the message three times before finally looking up at her assistant to say, "This isn't possible. I mean, it's possible. I just can't believe it. I really don't want to believe it. Humans have managed a way to survive for thousands of years on Earth. Who knows how many potential extinction events they may have survived? And now they're on their way here."

"We have authenticated the message, and it is in fact from Earth. It must have been sent almost two hundred fifty years ago."

"Who knows what other space travel technology they have developed since then? They could be almost here for all we know."

"There's no way to really tell. It would be inconceivable to think that they could travel at the speed of light or even achieve faster than light travel."

"We would have to assume that they could show up at any moment."

"The message didn't mention when they would arrive?"

"That's all we have at the moment."

Victoria was speechless and sent her assistant away as she mulled over the scenarios that could have taken place on Earth in the thousands of years since they had evacuated. She felt as if she were a doe grazing in a field in a clearing by a forest edge, striding along peacefully looking for acorns and nuts along the way. Unlike most deer before they are ruthlessly slaughtered, she knew that there was a particular hunter out in the wilderness heading her way. These other humans could be lurking out in the interstellar woods anywhere, waiting to make their appearance and conflagrate everything they had going on Cardea, just as they had done with Earth.

She knew that even though it pained her to think about, she would need to tell Isaac about the events that took place today.

Victoria approached the medical room where Isaac was presumably spending the last few days of his existence. She had visited him every single day since taking over as interim commander. He wanted to stay briefed on all events taking place, like he was still in the position of leadership.

"There's Victoria, the one who stole my position from me," Isaac said jokingly. It was much fainter and slower than previous days. Isaac had been in a rapid decline lately.

She sat down in the chair next to his bed and replied, "As always, here's the latest photography from the next generation of thrill seekers exploring our new land."

Victoria flipped through the images on her tablet. A video played in the middle of where Victoria had turned it off earlier. A squad of river-rafters had just gotten through what looked like a level four rapid to a calm part in the water where many of them jumped overboard to enjoy a nice dip in the water. They were swimming back and forth until some folks on the side of the river on rocks tossed them ropes to bring them back onto shore before the next difficult section of rapids.

"I still don't see you in any of them," Isaac commented.

"I'm only ten years younger than you now. I'm not the athletic person who followed you into the vast unknown decades ago."

"It feels like yesterday to me. Any fan mail today?"

"Well." It took Victoria a few moments to answer. Her heartbeat thundered in her chest. She wanted to race down the hall away from Isaac. She scrolled through her tablet looking for Isaac's fan mail to buy her more time on if she was going to tell Isaac about the Earth message. "I received a message today unlike any others you've gotten before."

"I'm old enough now to see it all. I don't think you could surprise me at this point. The only thing left for me at this point is to drift off into nothingness."

The words weighed heavily on Victoria. She looked out of the window and imagined the next crew from Earth shocking Isaac as they landed on their new home. The next crew kicking in the door and telling Isaac the message instead of her relaying it to Isaac herself.

"You're right. It's more of your adoring fans wanting to let you know they appreciate their original commander."

Victoria shut down the tablet, knowing that Isaac would be much more at peace than if he were to know that humans were still on Earth doing just fine, and some of them were heading their way. She wanted Isaac to die knowing that he saved the entire human race from total extinction.

Isaac closed his eyes for the last time as the heart rate monitor flatlined. His terminal hypersleep.

Extras: A Brief History of Events

1969 - The US landed the first human on the moon. This is a monumental, small step for mankind that would lead to the eventual possibilities of humans expanding their reach beyond the solar system. That we have a moon in existence at all may be the reason we took that first small step and imagined it was possible to explore the other planets and eventually interstellar space.

1972 - The last moon landing that was a part of the Apollo space program took place. Humans would not return to the moon for some time afterward.

1986 - Space shuttle Challenger disaster during launch.

2003 - Space shuttle discovery catastrophe during reentry.

2011 - US space shuttle fleet retired as confidence in NASA comes under extreme scrutiny. Astronauts now must travel to space in Russian Soyuz rockets.

2015 - First vertical landing of reusable rockets by a private company. This would greatly reduce the cost of space travel and allow a great expansion of the private space industry.

2020 - First private company to send astronauts to ISS from US soil. This would end the US' reliance on the Russian space agency for space exploration.

2021 - All civilian crew launched into space for the first time, opening space exploration to the masses. Multiple private space companies send private citizens into space jump-starting the space tourism industry.

2026 - Space balloon project begins, which greatly reduces the cost and increases the availability of private citizens to visit space.

2028 - NASA returns to the moon through its Artemis program and puts the first woman on the moon.

2034 - First catastrophic loss in the private space tourism industry, no survivors. Congress bans all private space tourism companies indefinitely.

2048 - Humans land on Mars for the first time. The trip is accomplished on a five-hundred-day journey, with the astronauts spending thirty days on Mars. All astronauts, including Mark Watney, make it back to Earth on the first ship back.

2050 - With renewed faith and public interest in space exploration, the space tourism industry returns.

2051 - US sends supplies and equipment for an extended stay on Mars.

2054 - First extended mission on Mars ends in disaster and all crew members are lost. All space tourism is once again suspended indefinitely.

2058 - Fully autonomous electric self-driving cars have completely replaced traditional combustion engine cars. There are still designated racetracks where you can drive classic cars.

2061 - Halley's comet returns and creates a stunning spectacle for everyone on Earth.

2068 - The cure for cancer is finally found and human life expectancy greatly increases.

2078 - Super volcano in Taupo, New Zealand erupts, changing the climate for decades to come and renews the necessity in humans being a multiplanetary species.

2097 - Bases and underground networks are established on the moon by all major nations.

2112 - Humans return to Mars for a 900-day trip, where the crew spends five hundred days on the surface. The crew makes it back safely and we now have a much better understanding of the effects of long-term space travel and living short-term on another planet.

2116 - With a renewed faith and public interest in space exploration, the space tourism industry returns.

2122 - Mars is continually populated by a small group of researchers, much like ISS in the late 1900s to early 2000s.

2134 - Halley's comet returns and creates a stunning spectacle for everyone on Earth and Mars.

2142 - The first permanent citizens move to Mars.

2165 - Mars reaches a self-sustaining population number. People continue to move to Mars from Earth; however, it is no longer necessary for its continued success.

2178 - Pluto completes its first full orbit around the sun since its discovery in 1930. Pluto is still not classified as a planet.

2194 - A new spacecraft is developed that allows for it to travel at 5 percent of the speed of light, opening up the possibility of visiting the asteroid belt and beyond.

2206 - An exploratory mission is sent to Ceres as a first step before considering a mission out to the moons of Jupiter and Saturn that might harbor life.

2209 - Halley's comet returns and creates a stunning spectacle for everyone on Earth and Mars.

2215 - First crew sent out to visit Europa.

2219 - First crew sent out to visit Ganymede.

2229 - A crewed mission is sent to explore Saturn's moon, Titan.

2238 - Tours allow anyone to explore the magnificent gas giants of the solar system.

2247 - A new method for cryogenics for humans is discovered that creates no negative side effects. This begins the heated debate on the possibility of using this technology for long-range space travel.

2249 - Lovell space telescope launches in order to search for exoplanets hospitable to life.

2253 - Jacobs and Bolden space telescopes are launched as the demand for the knowledge of exoplanets increases.

2259 - Tarax Corporation opens its doors as an interstellar space travel company.

2285 - Halley's comet returns and creates a stunning spectacle for everyone on Earth, Mars, and everyone traveling throughout the solar system.

2302 - First interstellar space mission launches to give humans the opportunity to expand their cosmic footprint among other star systems.

ABOUT THE AUTHOR

My main reason for writing this book was to increase the readers' understanding and excitement in space exploration and to help everyone realize space exploration is necessary for the advancement of human life as we know it. There have been so many inventions and discoveries that have been made, either intentionally or by accident, by various space programs that have advanced technology in space as well as increased our quality of life here on Earth. Government space programs have been an incredible force, although I believe it is necessary for the private space industry to take us to the next echelon. The timeline in this book is troubling when most people think about the progress that we assume we'll make in space exploration, and I'm hoping that this book will serve as a warning about our complacency. We need to continue the discussion of taking care of our own planet and the continuous innovations that will spread our footprint among the cosmos.

I am also writing this to encourage everyone who is interested in writing to just start writing and see where it goes. I grew up never really reading books and focused most of my attention on mathematics and science, so this would probably surprise everyone who knows me that I wrote a book. My bachelor's degree is in economics with a mathematics minor, and I never even used that to advance my professional career. I can remember it like it was yesterday, dreading the idea of writing even a three-to-five-page paper for my economics classes. I started diving into reading science fiction and science nonfiction books at the young age of thirty-one after a tough break-up, and it really kept my mind occupied and provided me with an escape from the world around me. Reading books has really taken over my life since then. I started out slowly, just writing little scenes and anecdotes, and eventually the words came from out of nowhere at every different time and situation during the day.

Exercising has always been a time when creative ideas would pop up in my head, so I thought it was important to include certain activities in the book and encourage everyone to work on their physical fitness and their mental fitness. I've been running for over a decade having completed a few half marathons and even a (virtual) full marathon in 2020 along with countless other smaller races. Some of my best running sessions were on days that I really didn't want to get started, either because of weather or utter laziness, but I persevered for the most part and the rewards have been worth it. Physical and mental well-being are completely interconnected.

I really don't identify with any of the characters here completely. There are certainly parts of my personal story with each individual character. I'm an avid traveler and had the goal of visiting thirty countries before I turned thirty, which gave me a wonderful perspective of different cultures and a more global view of the Earth. We're all more similar than we are different, and many people forget that when they are enraptured with the minutia of politics and global conflicts. I'm always on the agenda of continuous improvement in my personal journey in all aspects of life, and I try to be a better person than I was the day before.

This project seemed like a daunting and completely unachievable task; however, I continued to pursue this dream and followed it through to the end. I'm hoping that you enjoyed the final product. Leave me a review and let me know if I should write a sequel or start a series.

Printed in Great Britain
by Amazon